The Red Album

Stephen Collis · The Red Album

BookThug · 2013

Cover by Mark Goldstein
Copy edited by Ruth Zuchter

The production of this book was made possible through the generous assistance
of the Ontario Arts Council and the Canada Council for the Arts.

ONTARIO ARTS COUNCIL
CONSEIL DES ARTS DE L'ONTARIO
50 YEARS OF ONTARIO GOVERNMENT SUPPORT OF THE ARTS
50 ANS DE SOUTIEN DU GOUVERNEMENT DE L'ONTARIO AUX ARTS

Canada Council   Conseil des Arts
for the Arts   du Canada

LIBRARY AND ARCHIVES CANADA CATALOGUING IN PUBLICATION

Collis, Stephen, 1965–
    The red album/ Stephen Collis.

Issued also in an electronic format.
ISBN 978-1-927040-65-2

    I. Title.

PS8555.04938R44 2013   C813'.54   C2013-901269-9

PRINTED IN CANADA

Contents

Introduction

The manuscript of *The Red Album* came to me in the form of a PDF attached to an email from the poet and translator Alfred Noyes. When I opened the document it had neither title – other than the Spanish word "narración" at the top of the first page – nor author's name, nor page numbers. It was, apparently, a short novel in twenty numbered sections; closer examination revealed that it, in fact, had 19 sections, as it was missing a chapter 10, the sequence jumping from chapters 9 to 11. Noyes, in introducing the manuscript to me, claimed it was written by his friend Gloria Personne, and he wondered if I might take on the task of "more or less formally editing the manuscript for publication." I asked Noyes why he didn't do this himself, and he replied that he was probably "too close" to Gloria, and somewhat shattered by her disappearance. Besides, he argued, "you are better connected than I am." Connected to what, I wondered? Nevertheless, I undertook to at least *read* the manuscript before I dumped it onto the sizable pile of things-I'd-do-if-only-there-were-time-but-there-never-is-any.

What I read was both intriguing and infuriating. I wrote Noyes immediately to ask for the rest of the manuscript. He said I had it in its entirety. I asked whether there might not be a continuation, in Arabic, drifting around some Spanish marketplace. He demurred. I noted the mistake in chapter numbering, and he said there was no mistake: Chapter 10 was indeed missing from the finished manuscript. I then asked if he could at least annotate the manuscript in any way. Several weeks later I received the version that we now place before the public, with notes provided by Noyes. At my suggestion we have also included, in a section of "documents," related materials that may lend more substance to the text: a fragment of Personne's incomplete "autobiography;" an essay of my own; and assorted other texts that neither fully clarify nor further obscure the matter at hand, but are certainly part of the "background radiation" shaping Personne's story. They could be approached as archival materials that the author might have worked into the substance of her incomplete tale, had she been able to do so. Or perhaps they can be thought of as the endless afterwards and appendices that fill out the scholarly editions of otherwise slight classical works. At any rate, it at least makes for a more fulsome publication, and possibly allows the story Gloria has left us some intellectual room to continue to resonate in the reader's mind.

About Personne's disappearance, no new information has come to light, other than a brief note she apparently sent Noyes: "Gone to La Ciudad." It is, for obvious reasons, a difficult time there, especially with the embargo and visa freeze in the aftermath of the revolution. Little information gets in or out right now, and apparently no one has heard anything from Personne since her disappearance. As in many such situations – we can only, at this point, approach this as a case of posthumous publication – we are left with the text and the text alone. And the text seems determined to keep its secrets.

One is faced with an intriguing mystery here: does Personne's text prefigure the revolution in La Ciudad, and her own disappearance? In terms of pure chronology this would appear to be the case, with the revolution occurring more than a year after Personne apparently sent the manuscript to Noyes. What comes first, the artistic representation of the revolution, or the revolution itself? I suspect it is merely a coincidence – but what an eerie coincidence it is. Of course there is no "depiction" of a revolution here: the revolution stops the story. It occurs somewhere outside representation, necessarily; but if we are to take it seriously, we need our art works to bring us oh-so-close, even if they can't take us directly into the square where the uprising is occurring. Such a depiction awaits a different sort of author, a different moment of composition – one characterized by a liberty no one I know is yet privileged to enjoy.

There is one other suspicion I continue to harbour, which perhaps explains this text's having "predicted" the future. And this is that Noyes himself is actually the author of what we have agreed to title "The Red Album." (This was Noyes's suggestion, and it surprised but pleased me, since this was the title I had pondered for a book I had been unable to write). In this version of the affair, "Gloria Personne" is no one other than Noyes's avatar, created to hide his poet's ambition to write a novel – still the genre that seems to mark one as a "real" writer; poets are always asked, infuriatingly, "but when are you going to write a novel?" the subtext being, "when are you going to grow up and write something people actually *want* to read?" In fact, when a poet writes a novel, something desperate and unflattering has no doubt occurred, which the poet is likely to shamefacedly attempt to hide. Noyes himself was silent when I asked, carefully, about this. He then shared with me a lengthy email correspondence between himself and Personne, in which they discussed everything from mushroom picking in the

French countryside to the architectural applications of "swarm theory." But then, nothing is easier nowadays than to falsify someone's digital existence. How does one return to notions like the "authentic" or the "sincere," or for that matter, the "committed" – and I mean these in both the personal and political senses – in this age of thorough dissembling and pretend "realities"? It is a question I am unqualified to answer.

My hope is simply this: that this story and its related documents might be of interest to readers, and that in reading, we may continue the work of Gloria Personne and, through her, that of the poet Ramon Fernandez, in whose similar disappearance Noyes and I have long had an interest. Someone once told me that "all real creators must eventually go missing; their abandoned and incomplete works are then left for others to continue, or they are of no consequence at all." And so I have always thought of writing and reading as continuing unfinished projects. Dear Reader, please continue with us a while.

– Stephen Collis

1 · Narración

1

After spending an uncomfortable night in the Girona airport, Dioscoro Galindo took an early bus into Barcelona. He sat near the front of the almost-empty vehicle, his head resting against the large window, vaguely aware of the landscape sliding past – farm houses, trees, ruins, a castle on a hill some kilometres across a long, low valley. Dio, as he was usually called, only came to (more or less) full consciousness as the bus wound down a hill, past the sprawling Estrella Damm brewery, and into the city of his ancestors (this is what he told himself) – his first ever visit to the old world.

Moments later he was sitting on a bench in a small park a few blocks from the bus depot, watching two children play. The ground was mostly dirt but there were some fairly new and brightly coloured structures for the children to climb on, which they did with gusto, their parents sitting on a bench across from Dio. Presently a large group of school children arrived and displaced the first two, or swallowed them up in their whirl of voices, feet and hands. Dio absently tried to pick out the original two, but couldn't. Maybe he fell asleep for a few minutes, he wasn't sure, but suddenly he saw the original two girls with their parents, surrounded by the school children and talking to, presumably, their teacher. There seemed to be some problem, and Dio had the impression the parents of the first two children were foreigners – they weren't speaking Spanish, anyway, and the teacher didn't seem to understand their complaint. The foreigner's children were visibly upset, crying or frowning, and the crowd of school children alternately smirked or looked concerned. Suddenly one of the school children produced a small, plastic toy, which was given to the foreign girls, who were much relieved. The groups parted, the school children back to their games, and the foreign family to their bench, where they gathered suitcases and, with one last look around, walked on into the city.

Soon Dio moved on too, crossing a broad tree-lined avenue and strolling, his suitcase in tow, its wheels hopping the uneven paving stones, into the narrow streets of the Barri Gotic. He was also a foreigner here. A tourist with suitcase. Someone from the colony (he thought the foreign family were probably Americans, but wasn't sure). His thoughts trailed off as the narrow streets and shadows took him in and he wandered aimlessly, not even thinking of where his hotel was, or of the tourist map he'd picked up at the bus depot and crammed into the back pocket of his jeans.

He could almost – if his hands were free – have touched both sides of the narrow street. Above him, the balconies, similarly, almost touched, the laundry that hung from them billowing out so that a shirt sleeve on one side touched the hem of a dress on the other.

Every once in a while a small car came barrelling down the alley, its horn blasting, scattering pedestrians into doorways. Dio witnessed a woman in a burka almost lose a bag of groceries in one of these escapes, only to move on, unperturbed, after the car had passed.

In a small square dominated by plane trees Dio sat for a while listening to a fountain burble and watching a young waiter set white plastic tables and chairs outside a restaurant while a friend smoked, leaning against a wall and regaling the waiter with some long, apparently humorous story.

When he came to a large square, bright with sunshine in front of a cathedral[1], he finally remembered the map and self-consciously took it out, trying not to look too much the tourist, while groups of people around him spoke French and German and ate gelato, or took photographs of each other eating gelato. Dio quickly located himself on the crumpled map (not too difficult) and, much to his surprise, found that his hotel was right on this square, directly facing the cathedral (which was shrouded in scaffolding, apparently undergoing a major restoration). He stuffed the map (incorrectly folded) into the outside zippered pocket of his suitcase and hurried across the square.

The hotel lobby was small and dark, with potted plants and a flat-screen television. The clerk could not find Dio's reservation. He could tell by the way the clerk cocked his head and paused whenever Dio spoke that he was having an issue (or so Dio imagined) with his accent. Or perhaps trying to pin where Dio was from. What does it mean to feel your language is not your language? The clerk was old, tall and thin, with a hooked nose, very severe and arrogant, and so thin and pale that he might disappear into the cracks of the white wall behind the desk, or get lost amongst the papers in front of him. Finally the reservation was found, booked under the Association for the Recovery of Historical Memory, whose representatives had taken care of Dio's arrangements (not

---

1   The large square is the Placa de Seu, and the cathedral the Catedral de Santa Eulallia de Barcelona, a fact we will only come to know later in the story.

altogether thoroughly, Dio was finding; who knew the airport he was flying into was not in Barcelona, but in an adjacent town, Girona?). Once this was resolved, the clerk's demeanour changed from condescending to grave, and he quickly had Dio on his way.

In his fourth floor room, Dio threw himself on the bed without even looking around and began staring up at the ceiling, as though he had been eager to begin looking into its complexities. These consisted of: 1) a single, domed light, with the shadows of dead bugs inside it, and 2) a large crack running from the light towards the side of the room Dio had entered from. It was quite a long and deep crack – an earthquake? – and suggested something of the age of the hotel. Suddenly the entire hotel was divided in two by this vast crack, so that guests looked out from their broken rooms into a gap birds flew through and street noises entered and papers fluttered through the air, sheets billowed, and the clerk looked up at Dio from the lobby, as though to accuse him of creating this vast crevice in the middle of his noble hotel.

Dio awoke with a start and thought of his wife and daughters. He wondered if this was all just fatigue or the normal strangeness caused by travel. He had travelled before and not felt so ... not himself. Once to Mexico, and twice to California, to visit his sister in Carlsbad and attend a conference in San Diego. But on his second trip to California, he remembered, he had a difficult time at the airport. Disgruntled customs officials with stern expressionless faces and holsters heavy with guns. Questions, questions (they spoke perfect Spanish, only swearing in English – but everyone knows those words) – what did his sister do in California? Nurse. How long had she lived there? Twelve years. Was she legal? Pardon me? Was she a legal immigrant, did she have papers? Oh, yes, she had married a Californian. A Chicano? No, no an American. Don Reynolds. And your sister's name? Conchita Reynolds.

Incredulity. No fucking shit, Conchita Reynolds? Ah, yes. Is there a problem officer? And on and on it went. But this time – in Spain, the land of his forefathers and foremothers – it was a different kind of strangeness. A belonging-not-belonging. Well, maybe it had also been a kind of belonging-not-belonging in California, where so many of Conchita's friends were Chicano, and spoke a Spanish peppered with English which Dio could make out only most of the time. But going to California had no flavour of *going home*, as this time in Barcelona seemed to – though to a home he'd never even once entered, except in his father's stories and in old letters from his grandmother Guadeloupe, now long dead. Whose voice he'd practically never heard now filled the room saying *Dio, Dio, wake up – your father sent you and you must listen to what I say.*

When Dio awoke again, he was sweating. His head ached. The blinds were drawn and the room was dark. He had no idea how long he had slept. The digital clock beside his bed read 4:02, but this didn't mean anything to Dio. Lifting his head he saw a thin strip of sunshine coming through the crack in the curtains. 4:02 pm. Still somehow meaningless, as he had no idea what time he had checked in, or if this was even the same day.

Opening the curtains revealed a view of the square and the scaffold-clad cathedral, standing as though it had been under construction since the beginning of time. Everything was bright in the sun and Dio squinted, his eyes adjusting slowly. He saw narrow streets striking off in many directions from the square, and people – mostly tourists, Dio imagined – seemed to swarm everywhere. He followed one woman in a yellow dress as she wove across the cobblestones to the cathedral, stopped and turned at its steps, perhaps adjusting her hat or sunglasses (her hand rising, but being too far away for Dio to be certain of the gesture – it might even have been a salute), then followed along its front, and turned into an alley at its far corner, where she was lost in a knot of moving bodies.

The shower was cold, the water of an uncertain colour and odour. But it revived him enough to realize how desperately hungry he was. He dressed quickly and went downstairs with his hair still wet.

In the lobby, the clerk who had checked him in called his name. It had the air of someone being called to testify in court. Dio approached the desk tentatively, and was given a message on a piece of paper, which read:

Señor Galindo,

I hope you will find everything to your satisfaction at the hotel. I will be here in the lobby at 10:00 AM tomorrow (I hope not too early for you?). We can begin the reclamation then.

Yours,

Amy Godwin
Association for the Recovery of Historical Memory

Amy Godwin. Strange name for a Spanish government employee, thought Dio. The clerk solemnly asked if there was anything else he needed – Dio was still standing at the desk, holding the message paper.

No, no thank you.

Forgetting his hunger, he walked across the lobby and out into the sun.

The city was just coming back to life after siesta. The metal gates on storefronts going up. Cafés opening their doors. Dio wandered, watching where his footsteps fell, the unmarked impression they made upon the equally invisible yet somehow still lingering impressions of so many centuries of footsteps. At the entrance to a narrow street, Dio watched a car wait for a metal post, obstructing access, to descend into the ground after the car's driver had slipped a key card into a wall panel. The car drove through – into a street it could barely fit in – and the metal post, a yellow light flashing on top of it, rose back into place. Dio wandered on until he came out onto La Rambla, then followed the flow of tourists along the great avenue, past bird and flower kiosks and street performers pretending to be statues, their faces painted the same colour as their costumes, sparkling and metallic. Just off La Rambla, he found the Boqueria market[2], and began walking up and down its aisles, not sure what he was looking for, although sensing there was something to be found there. He stood for too long in front of a pile of fish he didn't recognize, trying to ascertain their nature, arousing the displeasure of the fishmonger. So he went back out onto La Rambla, and lacking any other necessity for being where he was, cut back through the Barri Gotic, hoping he was going in the direction of his hotel. Somehow he did indeed find his way back into the large square, where tourists still clutched gelato, and, retracing the path he had watched the woman in the yellow dress take earlier, only in reverse, quickly found himself seated at one of the café tables outside his hotel.

The waiter came to his table and Dio ordered some tapas and a beer, then stretched his feet out from under the awning's shade

---

2 This market probably dates from the thirteenth century, and was originally situated just outside the gates of old Barcelona (now known as the Barri Gotic, or "gothic quarter"). But such information is easy enough to find out, and hardly needs comment here. I have, though, myself stared into the faces of the fish mentioned here, and it is truly a disconcerting sight.

and into the sun. People came and went in the busy square. He wondered if Barcelona was always this crowded, or just here in the middle of the tourist area, or if there was a festival or something else afoot. A group of overweight people came up to the restaurant to read the menu. They spoke loud English, some of which Dio could understand, but he chose not to try to do so. His beer arrived and he took a long drink. He wished he had sunglasses – why didn't he have sunglasses? He remembered a rack of them he'd seen in the airport, a fashionable woman turning it round and round, shaking her head.

Nearby in the square, a man stood holding a large open book in his hands, from which he began to read loudly, looking up from his text periodically to glance meaningfully at people passing by or slowing to listen for a moment. It appeared to be a phone book. It was, at any rate, a list of names and numbers, although the performer read them as though it were Quevedo.[3] Shortly a police officer approached the man and he stopped reading.

After his tapas Dio ordered another beer. Then he became aware of another man drinking alone a few tables away and apparently watching him. In a series of casual glances, disguised as surveys of the square, Dio saw that the man was about his age, had a moustache and not much hair, and wore rumpled clothes. He looked like Dio must – tired, staring because there was nothing else he could do.

When Dio's beer was almost finished, the man called out.

Buy you another?

---

3   The name dropped here seems a little arbitrary, as though it were the first Spanish writer's name that came to the author. The name "Quevedo" fits no more appropriately than "Bustamente" or "Lopez-Vega" would have.

Dio looked around like he had not quite heard.

Buy you another?

Beer, asked Dio?

Yes, beer. The man smiled and nodded, holding his own almost-empty glass up.

Dio wondered for a moment if the man was a con artist of some kind – a crook laying in wait for unsuspecting foreigners and tourists, or simply a pickpocket trying to lull and distract him – but he didn't particularly care much at the moment. He turned his chair a bit towards the other man and shrugged.

Sure, let's have a beer.

The other man got up from his table and came to Dio's, lifting his empty glass in the air again and gesturing to the waiter. His smile seemed genuinely friendly, and reminded Dio of a colleague from his office back home. He introduced himself as Leandro, and Dio told him his name.

You are not from Catalonia, Leandro observed.

No. South America.

Leandro nodded his head, but didn't ask for any more specific details. I have never been, he said. Once to Madrid. Once to France. Several times here to Barcelona. Mine is a small Catalan town, Alcarràs.[4] I come here this time for my wife's illness. And you?

---

4   A small town to the west, about halfway between Barcelona and Zaragoza. Really, an unremarkable, circular stone village with fields sprawled around its outskirts and a river nearby.

Dio wasn't sure if he wanted a full catalogue of his travels (which wasn't much more impressive) or simply the reason for his present visit to Barcelona. He didn't really want to talk about the latter, so he simply said, Business. Again, Leandro didn't seem to want to know anything more detailed. There was a long pause in which they drank and stared out into the busy square. Eventually Dio thought it polite to enquire after the health of his acquaintance's wife. Leandro nodded enthusiastically.

She is doing much better, thank you. Now I am waiting for her re-covery. A few more days, the doctor says. Before, we were waiting many weeks for a diagnosis. First in Alcarràs. Then at the hospital in Lleida. And then here, at the big university hospital. Maybe you don't want to know, but it was the strangest thing. It began with a terrible headache – the worst she had ever had. So bad she could not get out of bed. Her mother tried some remedies, but soon we sought a doctor's advice. The doctor said migraines, and gave her something for the pain, which had no effect. My wife is strong, and never sick. So we were much concerned. Her mother, who is always at our house, kept taking me aside and saying it was brain cancer, it was cell phones. Even though we don't have a cell phone! My wife would simply say, There's something wrong with my head. Something wrong. We went to Lleida, and there my wife went truly crazy. Shouting in the hospital, cursing at people who weren't there, asking strange and inappropriate questions of doc-tors – I think it was doctors – who weren't in the room. She called me Filo and said, Get a hair cut.

Leandro laughed.

I have no hair, my friend, and know no one named Filo. She be-came frightened, staring into empty corners of the room, whis-pering. Her eyes, which I always thought were so beautiful, receded somewhere into her head, as though not wanting to see or be seen.

Leandro paused to finish his drink as the waiter brought two new beers. Dio wondered what he had got himself into, but with a full belly at last, and his second (or was it third?) beer, he didn't much care. If his new friend wanted to talk, Dio would listen.

She became violent, Leandro continued flatly, staring into the centre of the square. The doctor told me she was psychotic, or perhaps schizophrenic. In quiet moments my wife told me a small voice was talking to her, inside her, but she wasn't sure what it was saying. Baby talk, she would say. She developed a fever, then had a seizure. They sent us to the hospital in Barcelona, in an ambulance. She slept the whole way, and then for almost three weeks here. Coma. Her eyes would open, but she would not respond to any stimulus. Not even a sharp needle. I was sure she was gone for good. Prepared myself at last. Mourned the fact that she had not been able to have children – something that made her mother furious (her mother had eight children of her own – but my wife was the only daughter). The doctors, however, remained very curious – like my wife was a great mystery they must solve. They asked me many questions about my wife, the history of her health. What was this scar from? Had she always had this mark on her calf? Had she always had headaches? Nothing seemed to indicate what might be wrong. Scans, spinal taps. Nothing conclusive. White blood cells, they told me, indicated possible encephalitis, a brain inflammation, but they could find no cause. They wanted causes, above all. Believed in causes. A doctor would propose a theory (herpes – I would frown – lyme, syphilis?), but the other doctors (there were many, now, all so curious about my wife) would shake their heads no, no, no, nothing to indicate that.

Leandro took a long drink. His pauses were becoming dramatic, and he seemed to enjoy his role as storyteller. Dio wondered if he had been lonely all this time in Barcelona, with no one but doctors to speak to. Presently he began again.

You know, I have learned a lot about medicine through all of this. The doctors would speak, and then later, I would go to the internet café, and use a computer to look up the things they had been saying. Words I had never heard before. Really just sounds I would ask them to write on a piece of folded paper I kept in my shirt pocket. I understand things, now, about the brain I would never have thought. You know, the cells in your body are renewed all the time, they die and are born anew, so in terms of what you are actually made out of – flesh and bone – you are not the same you as you were five or ten years ago. Literally. Not one cell. You have been replaced by another you. And in the brain, even faster – not the same brain it was, maybe days, hours ago. Proteins dissolve and new proteins form. Synapses fire in new patterns. Now, how do we remember anything at all? Forgetting, *that* I understand. Especially now. It's obvious. But recollection, that's a mystery. You know – how hard would it be to break and replace a pitcher and not spill any sangria?

Anyway, out of desperation they did a CT scan of her whole body, and found a cyst on her left ovary. It is known as a teratoma. That sounds like the name of a Spanish town, but it means *monster* in Greek. This teratoma is small and smooth, like an olive, on the outside, but inside it may have a variety of cells and tissues – even growing hair and teeth. That's the monster part.

Leandro paused, smiling, to see how this sunk in. Dio nodded, frowning.

One doctor was convinced this was the culprit. The little monster was killing my wife. Ovarian Teratoma Encephalitis, that was her diagnosis. (This doctor was a young woman, and beautiful, from Madrid.) The little bastard had grown some primitive brain cells (*primitive* was what the beautiful doctor called the cells), and my wife's immune system had mistaken these for foreign cells and sent antibodies to destroy them. These antibodies then went on to attack the same kind of cells in my wife's brain. Can you believe that?

It's incredible, Dio agreed.

Incredible. And I started to think, if you can believe it, that that monster is the closest we will ever come to a child of our own. And my wife's body wanted to kill it! Because it had a brain. Or at least brain cells, however primitive. Would it have had thoughts? Feelings? Memory even? I wanted to ask, but didn't. The doctors cut it out, and my wife regained consciousness. Now she can go home in another day, maybe two – completely cured. I couldn't bring myself to ask – I wanted to, some strange enemy within me wanted to ask – if I could have the cyst – you know, like tonsils in a jar. A memento. To remember our little monster. But I couldn't quite say it. And the beautiful doctor was so pleased, so excited, she really wanted to get a good look inside our cyst – Let's have a look inside this guy, she said – so what could I say – No, give me the monster, I want to keep him!?

Leandro stared into his beer. Dio shifted uncomfortably, starting to think about his bed, the crack in his ceiling, his appointment tomorrow with the strangely named Amy Godwin.

It's an interesting story, anyhow, Leandro said apologetically. It raises so many questions for me. For instance, what do you think makes us human?

Dio shrugged, I'm not sure I understand your question.

What makes us different from animals? I'm not a religious man –
really, not much religion in my village since the Civil War, when
we shot the Priest, bless his corrupt soul. Darwin, from what I
hear, is right. We are animals. We eat and shit and fuck. We want
to reproduce ourselves, feed our young. Then we die. How are we
different from animals? Animals don't build hospitals, or cut each
other open to remove rogue cysts. They don't have complicated
names for their problems, or scientific literatures about those
problems, with definitions on the computer. They eat and shit and
fuck and die. So, in part, it's language, right? That we name things
and make those names our problems, the subjects of our literatures. But then I read on the computer about a dog who knows
300 words. There are 300 things his owner can name, or actions
he can command, and the dog knows and goes to get the thing
named or perform the action commanded. 300. And that's not all
– a parrot I read of, it said the parrot was smarter than the president of the United States! A joke, but the researcher, she's in Buenos Aires, reports that the parrot can express all sorts of desires
and feelings, and understands inflection, so the same word can be
made to ... to mean something else. Like the bird really understands language, how sound and meaning go together. Amazing.

I think ... I think it's that we think of ourselves as human, Dio
offered. Leandro nodded, and Dio went on. That we, you know,
think we're human – a member of that species, an example of the
category. That we're special and stand apart, or have a mission or
a cause or purpose. Whether we do or not. Just that we *think* that,
and think – like you said – What makes us this and not that? I
can't imagine sheep thinking about being sheep, or dogs thinking, Wow, it sucks to be a dog, I wish I could have a beer and
go to college. Only humans imagine what they are, generally, and

want what they don't have, things that go beyond mere survival. Desires. Imaginings. Dio paused, his hand counting things off in the air. At least, that's what I think. That it's just that we are given to imagining such things as categories and desires.

Good, Leandro nodded again. Good. Very scientific. Darwin. I love science. At home, I build things. Mostly furniture. I work with wood. Sometimes plastic and steel tubing (that's when I went to France, to get the tubing in my uncle's truck), but mostly it's wood. One has to be scientific to make a chair come out right, or a table to keep your cups and pictures from falling over. Or for it not to crack wide open. Measurement and design. Exactness. Occasionally my wife has found popular science magazines for me at the grocery store and I read them and I think. I like to know how things work. But it's only the past few weeks that I've been using the computer and I can't believe all the things I can read about science there. About time and the universe and how small and insignificant it is to be human and how the earth is warming up or how they built a tunnel under the water to England – that I would like to see. Do you have a computer Dio?

Yes. One at work and an old one at home. The home one is mostly for my kids. And my wife uses it too.

Leandro nodded. She must be a smart woman, like the doctor from Madrid. What work do you do?

I work for the government in my city. Urban planning. Mostly I work on green projects – parks, bicycles.

Bicycles?

Yes, bicycles. Improving bicycling by designing paths through the city, greenways for cyclists – and pedestrians too. It's a new program, a European idea really, which our mayor seems to think lends his administration credibility. Sophistication and forward-thinking. We haven't done much yet though, and we have almost no funding. But there are too many cars in my city, and the pollution and congestion is terrible as a result. So we want more people to ride bicycles, and for that we must make bicycling easier and safer. It's for the environment – global warming, like you mentioned – and for improving lifestyle and fitness, like it's better for you to exercise on a bicycle than to sit in a car all day. Better for the air too.

Your city must have a very liberal government. Socialist? No doubt. They care for people, and even the earth. They think scientifically, and that's good. We have a socialist government here in Spain once again too. But, not much changes in my town.

Dio smiled. Things change slowly in my city too. The government calls itself socialist, and even brings in liberal ideas from Europe, but … I'm not always sure what that means. Socialist. We have had right-wing and left-wing governments, but as you say, the difference is not always discernable at the local level. Usually what changes is how the government talks to other countries, to the United States, and the oil and mining interests.

Yes, that's important too, Leandro nodded enthusiastically, taking his next beer from the waiter. The café was crowded now, and the square still filled with people, tourists and vendors and performers. Even more people than before. Somewhere there was singing – a choir, perhaps; Dio couldn't see through all the people – but somewhere across the square there was singing, and occasionally, applause.

To talk to the United States in the right way, Leandro continued, that is what our good governments do.

Dio and Leandro fell into silence, seeming to have exhausted their conversation. They watched the crowd passing, and the other patrons in the café, many of whom were foreign. Leandro leaned close. This is what I love about the city, he gestured around them, speaking in a hushed voice. So many foreigners, like yourself, people from all over, the whole world, as though sending representatives here to Barcelona. I like that, like you said, members of the species, examples of the category *human*. It makes me feel scientific, like gathering data or something. Observing the characteristics of this animal, Man. In its natural habitat!

Dio nodded again, but Leandro shrugged, sitting back, and seemed a little uncomfortable for the first time. Then he suddenly took up another topic.

There is a town, in America, that was a mining town. Coal. And at some point a fire began in the coal seam, far underground. I can't remember how – I read about it on the computer – someone made a mistake. Negligence or some human carelessness, no doubt. But the fire has been burning there since the 1960s. Sometimes the ground caves in, and smoke comes out of gardens (where the vegetables have been cooked in the ground), from under sidewalks and collapsing streets. The sides of hills. Like they are living in hell, you know? Then, of course, they had to begin abandoning the town – only some old folks did not want to go, so they have stayed in the smouldering ghost town, alone and watching it fall into ruin. Coal fires burn slowly underground, where there isn't much oxygen. They think that the fire might burn for another two or three hundred years. Can you imagine? Three hundred years of burning! The earth on fire for whole lifetimes, while people walk around above wondering what souls are being tortured beneath their feet – what sins are being expiated. As I said, I am not religious – it is an opiate, right? – but it makes you wonder. The strangeness of ordinary things. The horrible and amazing strangeness of what really does happen. We don't even have to wish or imagine. It happens!

Dio did not know what to say. He thought about the fire burning underground, year after year. It made him think of end-of-the-world movies. Tidal waves. Deserts where cities once stood. Some child's toy left on broken, abandoned asphalt. It made him sad. He didn't like the idea of empty towns, of places fallen into complete ruin. Abandoned places. Ghost towns.

I would not go, Leandro began again. If it was my town, you know, I would be one of those old folks watching the forests and weeds take the town back. I would keep a watch on those fires. On the emptiness.

Dio nodded, then drained his beer glass.

Leandro sighed. I have kept you too long friend. He stood, downing his own beer, and took out some euros. But it has been good to talk to someone, and you have listened well. I thank you.

Dio stood too, and they awkwardly tried to insist on paying for each other's drinks. Leandro finally won the argument by insisting that it was his country, and he had to be a good host to the foreigner. They shook hands, Dio wishing Leandro's wife well, and they parted.

Back in his room, Dio resumed staring up at the cracked ceiling, as if his day and the strange conversation with Leandro had been a mere interruption of this more important work. He dozed and dreamed, and in his dream he was in a car driving through some city. Steam or smoke rose from manhole covers. Leandro's little monster was in the seat beside him, all teeth and hair, giving directions. The little monster began to talk like one of Dio's own daughters, about school and a play or something, about playing chess against a robot or computer which always won, no matter how hard the little monster tried, smoke coming out of its mouth in the effort, and then the creature began to berate Dio for driving a car when he could easily be walking or taking his bicycle. All these cars, it said, each with its solitary driver, burning for hundreds and hundreds of years the last drops of oil, and what are *you* doing about this problem?

When he awoke it was night. He looked out the window. The square was well-lit, and still many people wandered across it, less than earlier but still many, late-night revellers Dio assumed. He also noted the bicycles for the first time – bicycles the city provided and which anyone could use by putting a card of some kind in a box at the rack where they were kept.[5] He began to think of whether he could do this back home, and worried for the thousandth time about the terrible condition of the streets – so many unpaved or badly paved roads, potholed and decaying. Impassable on a bike.

Dio turned on the television. There were only a few channels, mostly talk shows. He watched one in which an older, Spanish

---

5   The program is called "Bicing" in Barcelona. They have a similar program
in Paris, where I have seen a woman in a business suit race one of these
bikes along the Rue de Sevres at high-speed, like she was competing in the
Tour de France, her nyloned calves pumping furiously. I know for a fact that
Gloria Personne is no cyclist (an inner-ear condition affects her balance) and
therefore, assume the inclusion of this element to be a pure flight of fancy.

man smoked and posed questions to two young women, who excitedly responded at the same time.[6] Dio couldn't make out what they were talking about – a party, it seemed. A commercial came on for a new drug a pharmaceutical company had developed for erectile dysfunction. It included a long list of fairly disturbing potential side effects, including receding gums and excessive hair growth.

Dio thought of Leandro's wife. Then he recalled a game he had brought his children back from California the last time – a game called *Operation*, in which you tried to remove small plastic bones and organs from the body of the cartoon character Homer Simpson.[7] When you hurt the patient, he yelled, *D'oh*, and other things in English that he said in the cartoon on TV. Dio's daughters loved it. Perhaps it helped them learn some English, Dio wasn't sure, but they certainly liked it and Dio's wife joked that maybe they'd grow up to be doctors. The game had playmoney which you earned for successful operations. How did people think up games like that? Why? Someone had to sit around and decide what Homer would say. That would be the easy part – you just had to watch the cartoon on TV. But at some point, people at the toy company had to sit around and decide: how much money should the kid earn for the operations? How much money do we need to put in the game? This is what bothered Dio as he thought about it, that someone had to have that conversation. That calculations had to be made to determine the amount of play money used. That time was taken up, meetings called and wages paid to designers and planners and other smart and educated people who sat about seriously and said, well, how much do you pay a kid for removing this cartoon guy's kidney? It made Dio feel uncomfortable somehow.

---

6   This may have been the popular news roundup show *Caiga quien caiga*.
7   I believe this is a variant on the original Milton Bradley game.

Like a problem he could not imagine a solution to. But then, the kids loved it. Until the pieces were lost and the battery wore out and Homer slowly sounded less and less like Homer, and then the game was put away with other games that had similarly lost their parts or worn out their batteries.

Dio wondered, should he go out, or stay in?

He found a football game on the television and watched for a while. He'd hoped it was FC Barcelona, because a famous player from his own country was on the team. But it wasn't. He wasn't particularly familiar with the teams and soon lost interest. But he didn't want to go out again. He was in Spain, he told himself, in the city of his father's birth. This was his first and probably the only time he would be here – he should go out, see things. See where his ancestors had lived. But he could tell already, just looking out at the cathedral behind its scaffolding, or the square where old stone walls, to the side of the cathedral, bore plaques and people stood and read and looked at tourist maps, he could tell, or felt, that history was a great weight here and people came to look at history like some thing that had been propped up and tickets sold to go see it and he didn't want any part of that, wasn't even sure he wanted any part of the history he'd been asked to come all this way to witness – the history his father had asked him to go see because he was too old and sick himself to go, and his son Dio would go on his behalf and represent the family and stand in front of history like some propped-up bit of old architecture and remark and be remarked, pay respects and bury what had been until recently forgotten or not even known at all. Something that had been dug up, and now needed proper burial – if only to keep it buried once and for all.

2

Dio received a wake-up call at 9:00 AM. Not remembering having ordered one, he rolled over to ask his wife, and was momentarily startled by the empty space beside him. He stared for a minute at the bedsheets, the light falling across them from the half-open curtains at the window.

He showered and went down to the lobby. He was early for the appointment, so he went into the café he'd been drinking in the night before and ordered a croissant (which struck him as a European thing to do) and a coffee. There were olives in a bowl on the table which Dio looked at while he drank his coffee and listened to the voices of people outside in the square. What was the square called? Dio didn't know. It was something like the main square, it must have a name – he could ask the waiter, but felt self-conscious about seeming foreign again. The cathedral square, he decided to call it. There was another cathedral in Barcelona he thought – he remembered its image from the Olympics – all spires and height – but this wasn't that cathedral.[8] So maybe there was another, more important square somewhere else?

At 10:00 AM he went into the lobby to wait. He watched people come and go. Whenever a woman passed, even if she was with someone else, Dio looked closely to see if she seemed to be looking for someone. Some men gave him strange looks. At 10:15 he

---

8   Dio here refers to Gaudi's Sagrada Familia, between whose spires in 1936 the anarchists hung a large, red-and-black banner. Orwell, famously, condemned the building as an eyesore (in *Homage to Catalonia*), but others have seen something more significant in the structure. Certainly Ramon Fernandez, whose acquaintance we have yet to make, saw soaring allegorical heights in the structure's incomplete spires. See Stephen Collis's essay, "The Plebian Cantos," in the *Documentos* section of this book, for further details on this.

went to the desk to ask if he had any messages. The clerk was a young black woman. She checked and yes, there was a message for señor Galindo from an Amy Godwin, who said she was running late and could they meet at 11:30 instead. Dio shrugged, thanked the clerk, and wandered out into the square, uncertain as to what he should do.

Across the square, Dio walked down a very narrow lane beside the cathedral, and then randomly turned down another narrow lane, in what he thought was the direction of La Rambla. Rounding a corner, he came into a small courtyard in front of a nondescript church. Several boys there were playing football. Dio looked at the church. The masonry around the wooden doors was pock-marked with holes, chips out of the sandstone. They had to be bullet holes, Dio figured. What else? During the revolution, per-haps, some soldiers or, what? Fascists? Must have been holed up in the church and the republicans (Dio was trying to remember what little he had read, or heard his father say), or whoever was trying to take over the city, had simply blasted them out of there. Amidst the boys calling for the ball and running back and forth, Dio tried to imagine the men in the doorway shooting out into the small courtyard, and the men crouched in the two alleyways leading into the courtyard, shooting back – the bullets spraying the church front and sending dust and pieces of stone into the air. Cinematic.

The confined space began to bother him, so Dio went back to the cathedral square. Other than the cathedral, his hotel and one or two other hotels, the square was surrounded by shops and restau-rants. Some of these sold the gelato Dio saw the tourists eating. He looked at his watch and made the calculation to Barcelona time: 11:00 am. (He hadn't bothered to change the time on his watch – he wouldn't be here long, he'd reasoned, and someone at work had said not changing your watch made the jetlag easier to deal with. Plus this way he could keep track of what his family at home would be up to.) Not really knowing why, he entered a small shop and bought a gelato (vanilla), then went back out into the sun to eat it, like the other tourists. Some Germans approached him and, in bad English (at least, Dio thought it was bad English), asked if he would take their picture in front of the cathedral. He pretended not to understand. They kept smiling, holding up their camera, and miming the photograph. Dio sighed and took the camera. The Germans arranged themselves. One of them – an old man with unusually tanned and smooth skin – held Dio's half-finished gelato, so he could operate the camera. Dio said, *Smile*, in English, and the Germans grinned. Dio returned the camera and retrieved his gelato and the Germans all said *gracias* and walked off talking loudly in their own language. Dio looked at his melting gelato and dropped it in a garbage can that was close by.

As he walked towards his hotel he saw a young woman standing in front of the glass doors, smiling. She wore a dark skirt and blazer and plain-looking shoes. Her hair was black and neatly styled and she wore makeup. Really, she looked very Spanish, and pretty, Dio thought, as she introduced herself as Amy Godwin (in perfect Castilian, as they would call Spanish here). (Dio thought he had heard Catalan spoken on several occasions – by the waiter's friend in the small square his first moments in the city, and in the gelato shop – but he wasn't sure.) He shook her hand and introduced himself, wondering, how did she know who he was? Amy Godwin gestured towards the café, the outdoor tables of which were just to the side of the hotel entrance, and they sat down.

After apologizing for her delay, Amy Godwin asked Dio questions about his trip to Barcelona, how he was finding the hotel, whether he liked the city and had he had time yet to explore much?

She had an excited, breathless way of speaking, leaning close and confidential. Perhaps she was nervous. Dio said no, he hadn't explored much yet, but yes he liked the city, though he thought there were too many tourists, and things seemed expensive (beer, the gelato he'd just tried). He was interested in the bicycles, he said.

The bicycles?

Yes. The bicycles you can rent and then leave near your destination, like taking a taxi, only healthier, more fun.

Wonderful. Amy smiled and her hands flitted about, as though conjuring things from the air. Yes, they are a new program and very successful so far. Many cities in Europe are trying them. In Barcelona, it's perfect – the Barri Gotic's streets are so narrow, no good for cars, but by bicycle, perfect. Even business people are using them. Tourists too of course. There is a saying the program is using in its advertising – *a bicycle takes you to another world.* Don't you agree?

Yes, of course, Dio said. Then, hesitantly, he asked if Amy was from Barcelona, and she admitted that she was not, but said that she had lived here for many years now. Before that she had lived in Valencia, where she grew up, but she had been born in England.

That explained the name, thought Dio as he nodded.

It's an interesting story, perhaps not entirely unlike your own, Amy said. My grandfather, an Englishman, fought in the Civil War. Like your great uncle. So we have that in common.

Ah, said Dio, but my great uncle was from Barcelona. Or at least … he lived here then. And my grandmother, his sister.

And your father emigrated, shortly after the war.

Yes, so I was born in South America. But my grandmother stayed here, alone. She did not want to emigrate, but thought it was best for my father. Because of … of Franco.

Dio paused, not sure if he had made a mistake in mentioning the dictator's name, or if that really was the reason his father left, or if he was quickly going to bore Amy Godwin with details she apparently already knew. He was also feeling his own uncertainty about a past he knew relatively little about, the details of which swirled in the shadows of cryptic and infrequent remarks his father made. So he quickly asked why Amy's grandfather, an Englishman, had fought in a Spanish war.

Amy told him that many foreign combatants (this was her term) had fought in the war – Englishmen and Canadians and Americans for the republican side; Germans and Italians for the fascists. Her grandfather was a young socialist worker in Manchester, and he felt it was a matter of class solidarity to go to Spain and support the socialist government there that was being threatened by Franco's coup. Volunteers went first to Paris, then by train to the border, and finally crossed the Pyrenees on foot. It was not easy, and you had to be determined to go fight the fascists – but many were. He fought first in Aragon, with the POUM.,[9] then briefly with the International Brigade, before he went back home to England, wounded. When Amy was a baby and her grandfather an old man, he wanted to return to Spain. He said he wanted to die in

---

9 The Partido Obrero de Unificación Marxista, with whom Orwell served and wrote about in *Homage to Catalonia*. In fact, many of the details about her grandfather that Amy offers here sound suspiciously close to Orwell's own experience.

Spain, where so many comrades had fallen, and now that Franco was dead, this seemed a possibility. My father was a doting son, Amy said, so he moved our family here. He thought it would only be for a short time until his father died, but my grandfather lived much longer than anyone supposed. We were five years in Valencia before my grandfather passed away. By that time, my father had bought into a prosperous orchard. My parents divorced (my mother did not come to Spain, thinking the move would be temporary, or maybe, you know, they both welcomed the opportunity and excuse to be apart, and they simply became ... used to each other's absence), and my father re-married a Spanish woman, who had been my nanny. I was in a Spanish school, and more Spanish than English. So we stayed.

Dio sat staring at the table and the coffee that a waiter had brought. The cup had a gold ring around it, and a chip right where Dio would have to drink.

Your grandfather must have been a man of great convictions, Dio noted.

I think the same was true of your uncle, Amy Godwin answered.

Dio shifted uncomfortably and made a vague gesture. He looked out at the square, then up at the sky where a few clouds lolled amidst the brightest blue.

My uncle ... my great-uncle, I did not even know he existed until your association contacted my father a few weeks ago. No one ever spoke of an uncle, or great-uncle – a brother of my grandmother who we left in Spain. No one. Not once. It's strange and ... it makes me think ... there was something to be hidden. Something no one wanted to speak of.

Amy told him he had nothing to be ashamed of, that his uncle (his great-uncle) was something like a hero, and that remembering him, in whatever details could be recovered, was the honourable thing to do. There is something like a secret agreement, she said, between past and present generations. Our coming was expected. Now, only now, could fulfillment be a possibility. Her voice became more serious when she said this, like she was quoting some significant and long-memorized passage. She straightened up in her chair, and her hands became still, and her voice more formal, like she was making a speech. Dio watched her, in part amused by the change that came over her. He saw that her eyes were two different colours, one brown, and one blue-green. Her nose might have been broken once. But it was pretty. A small accident on her face that led to better, unexpected things.

Dio looked out at the square again. A woman walked past pushing a stroller. Dio said that he didn't even know which side his great-uncle had fought on. Amy told him that he had been an anarchist. Dio paused a moment then asked which side that was. Amy smiled and leaned close again, her voice fast and confidential once more. He fought against Franco and the fascists, she told him. For the republic, Dio asked? Not exactly, Amy admitted. It was a little more complicated than that.

Dio did not know what to think. What did that mean, an anarchist? What did he believe in, this ancestor he did not know?

Does that bother you, Amy asked?

Yes. No. I mean – I guess I'm embarrassed to say that I don't really know what it means to say someone is an anarchist. I think of bombs and terrorists, nihilism, but....

Amy shook her head, straightened and shifted back into her speech-making voice. An anarchist – a Spanish anarchist – she told him, is none of those things. An anarchist here works towards libertarian socialism – a socialism without the state. Union organizing and direct action are the keys. If bombs must be thrown, or guns shot, so they must, but above all the anarchist believes that the means used to change the world directly affect the world one is changing it into. So if the revolutionary body is not directly democratic, free and equal, the society it fashions will not be either. This was their main difference from the Marxists. In Catalonia, in 1936, it was the anarchists who resisted Franco's army and socialized the state, more or less dissolving it. That had to be admitted. Her grandfather was a socialist, Amy told him. He believed the key was to wrest political power from the capitalists, and to hold onto it, with a firm hand, for the people. Socialists and anarchists often had the same goals, just different means of achieving them. Elections, party politics and vanguard parties are indeed sometimes guilty of the flaws anarchists see in them. Too often, as they say, our social democratic parties run their elections with the left hand, only to govern with the right.

Dio began to agree enthusiastically, to say that the same was true in his country, but stopped himself. It seemed somehow cowardly to badmouth the government that paid his bills.

Amy, still in speech-mode, became even graver. If we have become disillusioned, she said, it is no wonder. In Spanish countries – here, and in the new world – the tragedies are political.[10] There are assassinations, disappearances. Betrayals, organized robbery, the despoiling of the common wealth. Think of Chile, think of

---

10 I am sure I have read this in Eduardo Galeano – possibly in *Open Veins of Latin America*. But I cannot find it now.

Peron and Argentina. Guatemala. The long isolation of Cuba. The loss of memory – its forcible removal – all these governments have relied upon –

Amy stopped. Perhaps she could see that she was losing Dio, that his eyes were glazing over, his hands playing with the corner of the tablecloth. He had not even taken a sip of his coffee.

It is a lot to take in, she went on more quietly. Today we can do nothing. We meet and get to know one another just a bit. Maybe I will show you some of the city? Would you like that? That is the plan, anyhow. I am at your service for the entire afternoon. Then tomorrow, the formalities. In the afternoon we'll drive to the site where the remains were recovered, near Lleida, and then the following morning, we go to the cemetery for the interment. Does that sound satisfactory?

I guess so. Yes, sure, said Dio, nodding. He felt a long way away from his hands resting folded on the table in front of him. The ring on his finger. The full coffee cup and its dark contents. The white napkin close by, reminding him of his bed's clean sheets. The crack he kept returning to in the ceiling of his hotel room. The idea of sleep or the idea of a corpse in the ground and that long rest, as they called it, that endless sleep of the dead and their lack of anything at all to contemplate. Not even their absence from this world.

Amy, quiet a moment, seemed not to notice Dio's own distraction. Good, she said at last. Good. She had taken out a cell phone and began to stare at its tiny screen intently, her thumb working its buttons. A child screamed excitedly in the square. A suitcase was towed by noisily.

A cloud, Dio noticed, seemed caught on the top of the cathedral's spire, run aground there. Or anchored, like some ancient airship.

3

During a short walk through cobbled streets, and then as they walked idly through the rooms of the Picasso Museum, which occupied several centuries-old palaces, squeezed together in a narrow street, Amy managed, via a relentless series of questions, to retrieve from Dio the story of his father.

Ignacio was seventeen when the Civil War was over and his mother, Guadeloupe Fernandez Hernan, gave him what little savings she had and, a widow, sent her only son into exile in South America. There was, apparently, little discussion about the matter. And there was considerable urgency. It was a merchant ship that brought him to Buenos Aires, a reeking rusting freighter, and he had to work his way across, cleaning in the kitchen and serving the officers their meals, sick, almost always sick and stumbling on his unreliable legs. Staring at bleak, grey waters he had just, or was just about to, empty his stomach into. In Buenos Aires, family friends and distant relatives were to find him a decent job and provide at least temporary lodging (all had been agreed to in letters). They did neither. Ignacio (on his own initiative) found a job as a delivery boy, running almost anything on-foot (at first) and then bicycle (once he had enough money to buy one – Dio had always secretly thought that his father must have stolen the bike) between Point A and Point B, repeatedly getting lost in the city whose streets he did not know. Is this Florida Street or Corrientes Avenue? Which way to the Puerto Madero? How do you get from the Obelisco to the Casa Rosado? It's just around the corner? Shit.

In his first year, only one letter from his mother reached him –

this assuring him that she was well and expressing relief at the news from her friends and distant cousins, who had explained to her that Ignacio was well – working hard and being taken care of, fed a steady diet of empanadas. He was even growing fat! Marvelous. Much better than most Spaniards were doing at home under Franco.

Soon after this, Ignacio and some friends (lowlifes, one of the distant cousins, who had no idea, was later to remark) left Argentina for other parts of the continent (Dio could not remember if there was any particular reason to leave – political or otherwise). They wandered and worked in several countries – picking soy beans and coca, harvesting sugar cane and bananas, piling tailings at a copper mine – before Ignacio (a year, year and a half later) found himself alone in La Ciudad, jobless but with a little money from the copper mine in Chile, twenty years old and uncertain about what the future held, and yet calm, unworried.

Ignacio liked to talk about this time. A period of lazy days exploring a new city – new to him, and seemingly new to the world. A geography of potentiality. A space constantly rebuilding itself, starting over, as though it couldn't make up its mind how to begin, as though it wanted to know where it would finish first. A period during which Ignacio's strong but tired body recovered and filled out and his mind wandered with no purpose. Watched roads extending further each day into the jungle, where the city's edge progressed like a saw throwing off building-sized sawdust chips. Slept on beaches at Val Doro. Let himself out as a dance partner at a cantina called *Fortuna* frequented by old and lonely women who were said to be rich.

He wrote his mother for the first time since he left Spain. She wrote back and begged him to come home – things weren't as bad for their family as she had feared, and she could use his help. Ignacio wrote that he could not come home just now – that he had business prospects to pursue, opportunities, and could not leave the thriving, growing city he had only just arrived in.

Ignacio wanted to be in this place of beginnings, even if only to do nothing but watch it unfurl. It was like time-lapse photography. Like a flipbook. Only real.

During this time of the letters, he found work as a waiter in a slow café in a new and little-used street where the cook and owner slept in the kitchen, seemingly happy to wait for the city to wake up around him. Ignacio was mostly alone out front. He smoked and watched the street, waiting for it to come to life, for customers to appear – hungry construction workers or businessmen in too much of a hurry to have made their own breakfasts. Slowly, over months, it happened. Cars sped past and people strolled or loitered. Other businesses moved in: a laundry, a flower shop, a newsstand. Still the café was quiet and the owner slept and willingly paid Ignacio (though not very much) to watch the street. A girl who worked at the flower shop began to pass by the café window, her arms filled with orchids, her hands dirty and her earth-coloured hair falling into her face.

Guadeloupe Fernandez Hernan wrote again and sent Ignacio a yellow package filled with drawings. Sketches of animals and trees and a few angular faces. Drawings of cars and many airplanes and strange impossible vehicles of the imagination. Cartoon strips in little, square boxes, so small Ignacio could barely make them out. Inevitably someone getting cut in half, set on fire, or decapitated. Lots of decapitations (as though – neither Dio nor Ignacio would have said so – someone had been looking at too many Caravaggio's).[11]

It was with a shock of recognition that all this came back to Ignacio. As long as he could remember, he had spent his idle moments (even those moments he was supposed to be concentrating on school work) sketching and doodling and making up characters and cartoons and cars and airplanes. Stick men shooting each other. Castles under a rain of arrows. Ignacio laughed and scratched his head, sitting alone in the café, leafing through his childhood drawings over and over again.

He began to draw. On napkins or whatever was close at hand. Cars in the street, people walking past. The occasional customer. The flower girl with her arms filled with orchids. The flower girl more and more frequently, in poses Ignacio had never seen but now began to imagine – climbing a tree, sitting by the ocean with a large rabbit at her side and a radio in her lap, running from a jungle volcano with glowing red eyes and a red heart beating right out of her blouse.

This must be your mother, Amy observed, feeling smart and intuitive as she steered Dio through the gallery – the shush of sand-

---

11   One wonders at this comment, which seems a little self-conscious. Nevertheless, I have myself stood in front of Caravaggio's *David with the Head of Goliath*, in the Galleria Borghese, and pondered the painter's decision to use himself as the model for the dead giant's face. Maybe every artist at some point depicts his or her death in some shape or form. I do not know the significance of the reference here, though one does ponder the mysteries of Caravaggio's end (no one knows exactly where or when or under what circumstances he died, though die he did, in 1610, around the age of forty) in relation to the disappearances – around the same age – of both Ramon Fernandez and Gloria Personne.

stone and whispering tourists. Paintings Dio thought he should respect but didn't really understand or like. The faces all wrong. No depth. Grey and blue bodies.

Yes. But not the way you think.

Ignacio watched the flower girl and the flower girl saw Ignacio watching her. They smiled. Countless times, they smiled at one another through the window. Then one day (after months of inaction), he found the courage to step outside when he saw her coming. She stopped, flowers sagging in her arms like a small body, and they stared at each other for a moment. Ignacio gave her a drawing that he held in his hands. It was of the flower girl, holding flowers, just as she was at that moment. Same pose. Same expression. Only, in the drawing, she wore a New York Yankees baseball cap. She frowned, having to hug the drawing to the flowers in her dirty hands, crumpling the paper slightly and getting it wet. She said a curt thank you and, her eyes down, quickly went on into the flower shop. Ignacio, stunned, went back into the café.

The girl, it turned out, was married to the owner of the flower shop, Carcero Galindo. Galindo was nearly twice his wife, Muriel's, age. Ignacio learned this from the café owner, Pax, who grunted answers at Ignacio's awkward questions. What do you care, boy? Nothing, nothing, Ignacio said vaguely, carrying some dishes. You got a hard on? Pax roared. Ignacio shuffled away, staring at the floor.

Pax was a huge and indolent man. Ignacio wondered if he could even get out of the kitchen, imagining he lived there night and day, smoking and sleeping, wearing the small room like a worn and greasy housecoat.

Ignacio drew a sign for the café, which he placed outside on a sandwich board. He tried not to stare at Muriel when she passed, and she in turn tried not to look in the café window at the bored waiter. One day, a man came in to the café and ordered coffee and eggs. He wore a hat and breathed heavily through his nose, like he was out of breath, or trying very hard to smell something. When Ignacio brought him the eggs, he asked who had drawn the sign outside (it was a rooster wearing a chef's hat and carrying plates on its wings). Ignacio admitted that he had. The nose-breather nodded and asked if he wanted a job at his paper, *El Señal*. Doing what, Ignacio asked? Drawing cartoons – I need a new cartoonist. Last one left for Rio with one of the copy editors.

Ignacio had seen the paper, but never read it. He thought for a moment, then went into the kitchen to tell Pax he would have to quit.

*

Amy and Dio were in a large and brightly lit gallery on the top floor of the museum.

What are these paintings, Dio asked, gesturing around the room, which had brick walls and a high ceiling.

They are Picasso's variations on Velazquez's *La Meninas*, Amy said. There was a small reproduction of the original, to which she directed his attention. It is a great painting about painting. You see – Velazquez includes himself and his canvas in the painting, and possibly us too.

Us?

Yes, the painting's viewer, who is perhaps being painted – you see how the painter looks out at us, but his canvas has its back to us, preventing us from seeing what is there. But maybe we, standing outside the painting, complete it – or at least, take it into our lives beyond the painting. Picasso took this painting apart, here, on all these canvases, element by element. Studying its every detail.[12]

Dio nodded, looking around. Children and dogs. Birds and a balcony overlooking the sea. A dwarf. Much of it looked like cartoons, like a child's drawings. A shadowy figure in a cape stood at the back of one of the paintings. Dio leaned close to look, but a guard standing nearby cleared his throat, as two women, speaking loudly in French, pushed in close as well. Dio shrugged and moved away.

Like cartoons, he said.

Amy smiled. Your father was an artist too.

No. He would never have said that. He *was* a cartoonist. Then be became an editor, by accident.

Ignacio began drawing for *El Señal*. Drawings with little captions – people in the street making smart-ass comments to each other. Animals complaining about the weather, the condition of the roads, immigrants. He began to draw a small dog with a bandana – a street-wise character who always had something quick to say,

---

12 There are many interpretations – no doubt too many – of Velazquez's masterpiece. The one offered here by Amy is able, if not exhaustive. She focuses, for instance, on the withheld canvas, and the viewer's perspective, but she does not discuss the possible subjects of the painting – the king and queen – whose reflection may be portrayed in a mirror on the wall at the back of the painting. Perhaps there is a politics in this choice.

usually to someone who had done something stupid. Dropped a can of paint in the sidewalk. Slipped in mud on the street. Built a building with no door. The editor of El Señal – the man who had hired Ignacio and who always breathed loudly through his nose (his name was Dario Marquez) – began to receive positive mail about the dog cartoons, and he advised Ignacio to concentrate on the dog, which he had named Hernan. So he did.

Some readers thought the dog was a rabbit (because of its long ears), but it was definitely a dog. An underdog, who always came out on top. A homeless mongrel who roamed the city and played the smart-ass. Hernan acquired a friend (a fat chicken named Pax who lived in someone's broken-down yard and was always smoking a cigarette). There was also another dog, who was stupid and had fleas and got into trouble, so Hernan had to repeatedly spring him from the pound. A dog owned by a rich family would also make the occasional appearance, but only so Hernan could say something funny about the way it walked or its appetite.

Ignacio had signed his cartoons *Galindo* from the beginning. No one knew he was the increasingly popular cartoonist for *El Señal*. Marquez gave him a raise, and *El Señal's* circulation began to climb (it was the least widely read of La Ciudad's three daily papers). Ignacio had an apartment in a newer building. He bought a small, used sports car (which broke down all the time). He had girl friends (I know little about these women, admitted Dio – but there must have been women).

To make a long story short, after some ten years at the paper, a change happened. A new government came into power, and suddenly, in the new climate, *El Señal* generally, and Ignacio's cartoons more specifically, acquired new heretofore-unrecognized political meaning. The dog was a working-class hero, a dangerous proletarian dog. A government censor began calling Marquez regularly. Soon, this censor was asking to approve the cartoons before they went to press. Soldiers even arrived one day and insisted on speaking to *Galindo*.

What, my father liked to exclaim when telling this story, do they want to arrest Hernan now too?

Marquez was brought in for questioning on several occasions. Once, during a strike, *El Señal* was seized at the newsstands, and soldiers came in and stopped the presses. Marquez was arrested, and no one saw him again. Food for the fish in the river, it was said. No one else would take over the editorship of the paper (everyone was afraid). So Ignacio did, with a shrug. He knew nothing about running a paper, and this might have been for the best: he didn't know what he couldn't do, or what he shouldn't do, anymore than he knew what he could or should do. He put an end to the Hernan cartoon strip, turned the paper only towards the political centre (by dropping any article that dealt overtly with politics and concentrating on petty crime, entertainment and scandal), and while *El Señal*'s circulation numbers dropped precipitously, the government began to pay less attention to the paper. The name of the new editor, Ignacio Covas, was much despised, and people demanded to know where *Galindo* had gone. One of the many disappeared, no doubt. Workers drank to his memory, and government and police officials congratulated themselves on his silencing. In time the government changed again, and miraculously *Galindo* and Hernan reappeared. Ignacio had few friends, as he was what we would now call a workaholic, but he was prospering. He did what he felt he had to do to survive. He worked long hours. Occasionally, perhaps, he made love to his secretary, or took a woman no one had seen before to Santiago de Chile or Cartagena for a weekend. We can only imagine.

One day a woman came into the paper's offices and asked to speak to *Galindo*. Ignacio's secretary came into his office, with an odd look on her pockmarked face, said that a Muriel Heredia de Galindo wanted to speak to the paper's renowned cartoonist. A relative, perhaps, she smirked? Ignacio sat staring at his secretary, a pen in his hand marking the pause in the air, turning the name over and over in his mind.

When Ignacio came out into the small lobby, he stood and stared at Muriel for a long time. She did not seem to know where to look, glancing at Ignacio, then away into the corner, then at him again, then away at a potted plant. They knew each other despite the nearly twenty years that had passed.

She had the drawing of course, Amy said.

Dio looked at her quizzically.

Excuse me? Oh, no. It is romantic, I suppose. But not *that* romantic.

Over lunch, Muriel told Ignacio her story. Her husband had recently died after a long illness, during which medical bills had ruined their business. She did not know why she came to talk to *Galindo*. She did not know, exactly, that the cartoonist was the young waiter she had known, briefly, so many years ago. But there was something about the cartoon, the chicken Pax, and about the flower patch Hernan often tore up in front of a hotel (this was a running gag – really, a way of settling a score Ignacio had with a certain hotelier) that had made her, in a moment of confusion, despair and intuition, come to the offices of *El Señal* and ask for the cartoonist who shared her dead husband's name. Is your name really Galindo, she asked?

No, he said. It is Covas. Ignacio Covas. But I took the name Galindo for my cartoons ... I'm not sure why.

They were married, Dio told Amy, a few months later. Times were changing again, and a leftist coalition government came to power (this was in the late 1960s – a brief respite from dictatorships and right wing parties beholden to the United States), and *El Señal* was once again out of favour. Ignacio had little in the way of overt politics himself, though parties of various stripes regularly tried to gain the paper's ear, or claimed it as their fellow traveller, or damned it as the mouthpiece of their opponents. Ignacio simply wanted to make his living the way he knew, by producing entertaining, local, *straightforward* news. A paper without ideology, he liked to say.

There's no such thing, Amy interjected. She was using her official voice. To claim no ideology *is* an ideology – perhaps the most nefarious and pervasive one.

Suddenly she looked at him with a pained look on her face.

Oh – excuse me Dio – I only meant....

Dio shrugged. Sometimes his paper seemed too far to the right, sometimes too far to the left – all this depended upon the governments or the parties in question. Around him and his paper, the world kept changing – but it was all surface. The structure underneath never seemed to be affected. This time it was not *Galindo* who needed to disappear, but the editor, Ignacio Covas. So *El Señal* announced Covas's retirement, and the appointment of Galindo as the new editor. And Ignacio took his new wife's married name as his own new, legal name – more as a way of celebrating and cementing the restructured paper than anything else.

Of course it was an open ruse that almost everyone by now knew. It nevertheless managed to take the heat away from Ignacio's small, middle-of-the-road paper. The ascent of the popular *Galindo* to the editorship caused the paper's circulation numbers to skyrocket. It was a publicity masterstroke. Ignacio prospered. Muriel had a son (Dioscoro), and a year later, a daughter (Conchita). They were new parents in their early forties (Muriel had a son from her first marriage, now twenty, who came to work with Ignacio at the paper). Ignacio had never been so happy.

*

Dio paused while he and Amy exited the museum; they had barely looked at the paintings over the past half-hour. (This embarrassed Dio somewhat, who thought he had not shown enough attention or interest to please Amy, who had paid Dio's admission fee to the museum, and who was obviously proud of the collection and her city's connection with the painter.[13] Dio, of course, knew the name Picasso, and knew it was a famous name, but he had only limited interest in art.) They moved through the streets to a wider boulevard and Amy hailed a black and yellow cab (like a bumble bee, Dio commented) that took them to Parc Guell. There they walked amongst pine trees, silent for a time, under stone arcades and along flying rocky buttresses that formed terraces that seemed prehistoric plants turned to stone. Eventually they sat on

---

13   It is a strange connection: Picasso was not born in Barcelona, and only lived
there for a few years, in his teens and early twenties. Like Amy and Dio, he was
in some ways an exile, displaced. But I pass over these details as being of only
relative significance. The museum is indeed there in the city (with perhaps
a less impressive collection than the one in Paris), and it is filled with light
and warmly coloured stone. I have passed pleasant hours there pondering
the poetry of Ramon Fernandez and grammatical intricacies of Spanish and
Catalan.

a long bench covered in winding mosaic patterns and looked out over the city below them.

Why, Amy asked, did your father never come back to Spain? Why did he not return for his mother's funeral? I understand he is old and sick now, and sending you in his place makes perfect sense, but why did he not come for your grandmother's funeral, which was ... almost thirty years ago?

Amy was looking down at her feet, which must have hurt (Dio's did), while Dio looked out at the city through the haze, thinking.

Ignacio received letters from his mother infrequently, and wrote back even less frequently. Muriel, however, kept her better informed. They even spoke on the phone once in a while. And when I was old enough, I wrote her a few times too, and talked once on the phone. She cried and said my name, mostly. I'm not sure why my father turned his back on her, and Spain. He almost never spoke of it. With me, it was football or the funny pages, or these stories I've been telling you – stories of how our parents met, which are the sorts of stories young children love to hear. But he did not often speak of Spain or his childhood.

Dio stopped. He had spoken about himself too much – more than he ever had to a stranger. Maybe more than he had to anyone ever. Maybe it was the difference of being here, in Spain, as it were – in the past. Like some sort of regression therapy, as they called it. He coughed and looked at the city. Amy pointed out the vague spires of the Sagrada Familia, the construction cranes looming amidst the towers like arms reaching up to pull the spires down.

They walked across a square and under another arcade where the ceiling was a mosaic sky, suns and stars bursting amidst blue and white tile. On the way, Dio managed to ask Amy about her family. She told him about her grandfather in England and her father who, while a dedicated son, did not agree at all with his father's politics. They argued and then made up, again and again, resorting to ideologically charged jokes and insults. She spoke of this and many other personal matters that Dio would soon forget as a taxi took them back down into the city, to the Sagrada Familia, which stood like some cross between a spaceship and a coral reef amid traffic and tourists. Amy explained how the building had been left incomplete by Gaudi, who died in the 1920s, and how, after Franco had died and Spain became a democracy again, plans to finish Gaudi's church had been resurrected. Now, in another fifteen years or so, almost 150 years after construction had begun, the church would finally be complete, and the architect's vision realized.

Dio wondered about projects like that – projects that would outlast any of their original creators or planners – projects that did not depend on any one individual's life or lifetime. It was a commitment made by a community, the imagination of a future which one would not live to see. He found it hard to imagine anyone in today's world committing to such a vision. Did it depend on religion? He hoped not.

Dio looked up at the soaring spires, like giant tree trunks, and Amy said that sometimes she though it should remain unfinished, that things like this meant more when they were incomplete, like ancient ruins which would lose their mystery and magic if they somehow returned to whatever their unknowable original finished form had been. Not everything adds up, its every detail brought into meaningful relation with the whole. She said that more memory gathers around the broken and sundered. The pyramids in Egypt and Mexico had once had smooth, painted exteriors. They were the equivalent of today's glass office towers and huge television screens showing models prancing above the city streets. They are better half-eaten by time and failure.

Dio laughed as they sat on a bench across from the great structure, watching cranes turn behind the towers and tourists stream past. He had no urge to go inside the cathedral, and Amy did not seem to be about to suggest they do. A kiosk to their left sold postcards. Several hawkers tried to sell colourful trinkets, plastic toys that glowed and made horrible sounds as they whizzed into the blue air soaring with spires. There was a small, white cloud to the left of one tower. A bird cut across it and disappeared behind the Sagrada. Dio imagined taking a photograph and just managing to catch that bird mid-flight, about to disappear behind a spire, frozen in that moment forever.

Whatever *forever* meant.

You still haven't told me why your father would not return to Spain, and why he would not come to his mother's funeral.

He did not come, I think, because he could not, Dio said.

This was after the coup, during the dictatorship of the 1970s, when, Dio told Amy, he was twelve years old, his sister nearly eleven. Ignacio had got into the habit of going for a Sunday drive across the border in recent years – they were not far from the border in La Ciudad – and he could pick up some papers there that were banned in his own country, or he received packages and information that would have been more difficult to acquire in his own country. (This is what Dio said, though who knows how much this story was his own invention – or his father's. It's strange, this Sunday border-crossing; perhaps it happened once, and time and intensity of feeling had expanded the singular event into a recurring pattern. To in some way *naturalize* it, give it some glimmer of the mundane.) He thought this would have had to stop with the coup, Dio went on, but every Sunday he still took his family for this drive over the border, and every Sunday the border guards continued to let him in and out of the country with a smile and a nod. He had been at the height of his popularity in these years, years in which *El Señal* was second in circulation only to the leading socialist daily, and when calls of *Hernan!* often followed Dio's father (as he had become inseparable from the beloved dog for many people). (This, too, seems a child's invention.)[14] The dictatorship began to censor the papers, closing the socialist *Documento* altogether, and forbidding Ignacio from running the Hernan cartoon (a decree with which he complied, always willing to do whatever it took to keep his paper running). The offices of *El Señal* and the Galindo home were watched around the clock by soldiers in Jeeps (a detail which could come from almost any movie dealing with South American politics). They were all afraid that something would happen to Ignacio, as many people were beginning to disappear, or turn up dead in dumps and along the river and under the freeway near the shantytown. And still somehow the Galindos (if the story is true) were allowed to cross the border every Sunday and bring back their banned newspapers and smuggled documents. Like they had a special concession. Then one day, that changed.

What is an event? What makes what happens remarkable, memorable? Is it the cinematic intensity, suddenness, and surprise of

---

14 It is worth noting the incongruousness of these parenthetical intrusions. Were I the author's editor, I would recommend removing them. And yet I admit I am heartened by the voice I hear in them. [Collis note: we discussed this, and agreed to leave the remarks in the manuscript, despite the fact that they may have been the mistakes of a novice writer – a lapse in narrative control.]

the unexpected happening? *An event is anything that happens*, a philosopher contends. Is there anything more innocuous? Each and every day some range or set of things occurs. We do not mark all of them as *events*. An event has to do with the coming into being of the future. Events are changes, midstream. The past hurtles through the moment of the event, into the future, leaving the present both frozen and fluid. It is into such a moment that Dio attempted to descend now.[15]

I remember everything in the car that day, he said. I can see the comic book newly purchased in the store across the border (it was *The Mighty Thor* and a caption on the cover read *The Day the Thunder Failed* and it showed the god/hero with his arms and hammer raised to the sky).[16] I can see my sister with her nose in a novel, chewing her nails and oblivious to the car's jolts and bumps. I can see my mother's dress, which was yellow with white polka dots, the back of her shoulder and her hair, earthy brown but streaked with grey, neatly combed and falling to her shoulders where it curled up and out. My father had a grey felt hat on. I had my window wound down partway, and I can feel the breeze, and smell the river where the border crossing is at a bridge, and I can still feel the fabric of the seats in that car, plush but coarse, polyester, and smell its interior (some kind of air freshener? Menthol cigarettes?) and hear the distinct sound of its turn signals (a slow, deliberate, double-*plink*). We approached the border, slowing, as

---

15   I wish I knew to which philosopher the author refers here, but I do not. It is another awkward intrusion. I can only surmise that this section gave the author some difficulty. Perhaps, if she were here now, she would allow us some careful editing, or at least justify her choices.

16   That there is a Spanish edition of this comic book surprises, but there are no end to the surprises the modern culture industry throws our way. The Spanish title of the issue in question is *El dia que el Trueno no*. I myself once collected comics, but it seems a very dated hobby now.

usual, rolling towards the guards, our country's guards, who stood at the gate with machine guns cradled in their arms. I saw nothing strange. Heard nothing out of the ordinary. A bird maybe? The river? Maybe a voice called something out, I'm not sure. Then suddenly the interior of the car was alive with shattering glass, exploding and tearing open, like it was trying to rip itself – and us – to pieces, bullets flying past us, piercing the car's body or shattering windows, one I distinctly felt brush my arm and graze the comic book I held, knocking it from my hands before entering the car seat beside me, and another, passing from the front, came close to my head, perhaps even through my hair where it hung long and curling over my ear. I felt them pass. Like blasts of air. Like whispers of the devil. The car rolled and bullets kept passing through it and glass kept exploding and falling and I couldn't hear screams or yelling or anything human. Until the firing stopped and our car came to a stop against the border gate and the engine whined then stopped and steamed and hissed and then everything was quiet.

Amy waited while Dio looked up at the spires of the Sagrada. What were the words set there at the top of the spires? Who was meant to read them?

Dio and his sister were fine. Untouched. A miracle, some would later say. But his mother was killed instantly when a bullet entered the middle of her forehead. A clean and remarkably small hole. Other bullets hit her too, but the one in the head killed her instantly. Ignacio was shot seven times. At the hospital, they did not think he would live. They operated. Then he was in a coma for several weeks. Then, finally, he regained consciousness, and began to heal. But he never walked again.

I remember so little of the aftermath, Dio said. How did we get to the hospital? Who took us there? If we were to be killed, why didn't they finish us off? I remember being at the hospital, waiting with some people from the paper – maybe my step-brother, who would soon leave for America, and my sister, still reading her novel, its yellow cover spattered with our parents' blood. I remember holding a paper cup in my hands and feeling it slowly dissolve, the water softening it relentlessly as I rubbed and worked and worried it between my fingers.

Dio stopped and shrugged.

They sat a while longer, then walked into a subway station near the Sagrada, descended into the heat and smell, and rode the train back towards the Barri Gotic. Then they walked through the narrow streets to Dio's hotel where they stood looking at the square. During this time they barely spoke, both lost somewhere in thought. Amy occasionally pointed out some sight or landmark, but only half-heartedly. Finally Dio spoke again.

My grandmother died while my father was convalescing. Really, there was no chance to return, even if he had wanted to, which I'm not sure he did. Not sure, at least, until he asked me to return here to claim his uncle's remains. His uncle, whom he had never once mentioned to me, in my entire life.

Amy looked at her phone, then back at the square. The newspaper, she asked, *El Señal*?

He quit. Retired. The government claimed he had tried to flee the country, to drive his car right through the border gates. Run the guards down. That they had had no choice but to shoot. My step-brother was going to take over the paper, but then he did flee the country. Cut all ties. I've never seen or heard from him again. I think he went to America, but I don't know. My father's old secretary, Amelita, moved in and took care of Conchita and I. Ignacio … did nothing. He read (novels – no newspapers anymore). Cheap paperbacks. Adventure or fantasy stories. Mostly he watched football on the television. Game shows. Soap operas. But he rarely spoke and he never went out. He ignored the world around him, and was ignored in return. I was heading into my teens, so I ignored him too. Eventually Conchita went away. She worked in a hotel in Cancun, met an American, and moved to California. I eventually went to the university. I thought I would study architecture – the school in La Ciudad is highly regarded – but I did not have the grades for the program. I studied civil engineering instead, for a few years, and continued to live with my father and Amelita. Eventually I dropped out. But then old allies of my father's – men who had grown up reading Hernan – found out about me and got me a job with the city, in the small and underfunded urban renewal division.

And there, Amy Godwin, you have my story.

They stood awhile longer. Dio wanted to sit. He wanted to lie on his bed and look up at the crack in his hotel room's ceiling. He wanted to sleep then eat, then maybe, to listen to Leandro tell strange tales of his wife again. Or he wanted to be home again, and making love to his wife while a green and lush world waited outside their bedroom window.

4

In his room Dio thought about travel and meeting people you would not meet had you not travelled, and about how a body could have its movements mapped and how those movements would be very prescribed and predictable for the most part: to work, to home, to work, to the store, to home, to work to pub to home. The daily fight for the crude and material things of life. But then one travels to another land and the body experiences a sudden expansion towards refined and spiritual things and a line shoots out from home to airport to a place far off the map of the everyday, exploding the bounds of what had been known and assumed before, a radical shift in scale.

He thought of the moment the plane turns slowly onto the runway and the pause there, and the sound of the engines and then the sudden roar and the G-forces pushing you into your seat. The moment you are hurtled off the map, looking at the strangers around you also being thrown off their maps, all of them just a little shocked or surprised and uncertain, their heads turning in unison towards the line of the horizon just barely visible through small windows on the sunny side of the plane.

After a shower, he lay on his bed and thought of Leandro and his wife once more and the things he'd seen that day, and how he would describe them to his wife who had never even been outside of La Ciudad and its surrounding area. The curtains fluttered, his window open. His wife was making eggs, beating them with one hand, holding a book in the other, and then turned to explain something about the book, which Amy had apparently written. Dio might have responded, but then Amy was serving him the eggs and asking whether he liked historical novels. What, Dio asked? Historical novels – novels about historical figures and events. Things that actually happened in the past, and then are rendered in fiction. No, said Dio, no I don't think I do, I don't think I've ever even read one.

5

After a short nap, and then having something simple to eat in the hotel (some rice and vegetables with some sort of fish in it), Dio went out and walked through the narrow streets, watching people and catching snatches of conversations. It was evening and a certain lassitude had fallen upon the city. People were putting bottles in recycling containers. Old men talked on corners. A woman scolded a cat from her second-floor balcony. Above her someone took in laundry, sitting in a windowsill and talking to an old woman in the building across the street. Young men and women smoked and laughed in front of a bar.

Dio came upon the bullet-riddled church again, and again contemplated its façade. A saint of some sort was carved into the lintel above its black doors. Or the Virgin. Above her, a small round window. And above that, the arched roof of the little church.

How could he be sure they were bullet holes? He had certainly seen bullet holes before – there were plenty of shootings in La Ciudad – but never in sandstone. This seemed to make a difference. They were like potholes on a vertical street. Or craters on the moon. All splattered around the doorway. Clearly, someone or something in the door had been the target of a good deal of shooting. Men had died here, that was certain. On these very cobblestones. Died for words and their definitions. But their flesh and blood left no mark now. Only the bullets. Dio had read in a guidebook in his hotel room of another church – an ancient church from the thirteenth century – in which anarchists had piled up all the pews and confessionals and lit a great fire. Apparently, you could still see the smoke-stains on the ceiling of the great vault. Dio wondered if he wanted to go see that, but couldn't decide. Did one go to see the marks left by revolutionary fires? Was that tourism? What sort of political meaning could reside in some marks left by smoke?

He looked around, remembering the boys playing football. Tried to picture them, to remember how they looked, what colour their shirts were. But he couldn't even recall how many there had been. And this was just the day before. Four? Maybe five? As young as his daughters. Then he remembered something he'd read once – where? – he wasn't sure, but the words came just the same – *The true picture of the past flits by.*[17] The past, Dio thought, looking around once more, of seventy years or seventy hours ago.

Leaving the small, shadowed square, Dio heard a commotion ahead. Voices were yelling somewhere and a boy on a small bike sped past on a cross street, peddling hard, a woman's purse clutched in one hand. Then a woman, yelling, ran after, as best she could in heels. Dio rounded the corner in time to see the scene unfold.

The boy rode down a slight incline. The woman and other people in the narrow street were yelling and waving their arms. Suddenly, further down the street, a man leapt out of a doorway and into the boy's path. Dio watched the collision. The man who had lunged out collapsed in a heap with the bicycle. The boy and purse flew into the air, then crashed down several feet past the man. People crowded around the man who had stopped the bike, who appeared to be in considerable pain, though grinning and perhaps even a little jubilant, like a football player who had just headed a corner kick into the net, and took a boot in the leg to do so. Dio approached and saw that the boy was still on the pavement, with no one paying much attention to him. The woman in heels, now limping visibly, removed her shoes and walked past the collision

---

17 The quotation is so generic, it could have any number of sources.

scene in her bare feet. She picked up her purse, cursing loudly, yelled and gesticulated over the boy's body, looked at her purse as though it might be damaged, then turned and stood over the injured man, showering him with thanks and praise, which he accepted, still grinning and wide-eyed, sitting in the street while others crouched around him. It looked to Dio like his leg might be broken. A group of men picked him up, all talking at once, and carried him into the building he had rushed out of, groaning lightly but still smiling.

A crowd remained near the motionless boy, arguing and telling each other what they had seen, but not one was checking on the boy's condition. Dio came close and looked. He couldn't see the boy's face, which was against the paving stones, obscured by his long hair. Maybe it was a girl? Thin arms and hands revealed brown skin. Or maybe he/she was just dirty? There was blood on the street near his head. Not much, and Dio didn't think the boy was dead, but he was injured at any rate. Knocked unconscious. A wave of disgust came over him, as still no one approached the boy. There he lay, like a rat crushed and dead in the gutter, its teeth and little claws sticking out. Point and move on, stepping around the little monster. What made this boy a thief? What strange destiny brought him to this? Who made purses and put money in them and then left boys with nothing but bikes to ride and hands to grab? Dio wanted to squat down and touch the boy's back, maybe turn him over, feel his pulse, but his knees went weak and his stomach sunk and he suddenly needed to find a bathroom very badly. His skin crawled. Two police officers finally arrived, the crowd pressing around them to make their report, and Dio stumbled away in a cold sweat.

6

In the morning Dio met Amy in the lobby and they took the short walk to the Generalitat.[18] In doing so, they passed the alley that led to the bullet-riddled church, walking past the site of yesterday's bicycle accident. The street was clean and almost empty. Dio could hardly recall what had happened there. He half-expected to see a chalk outline of the boy's body, or a bloodstain, or a bouquet of flowers. But there was nothing and Dio wondered if he'd been awake or dreamt the whole scene.

In the nearby Placa St. Jaume, tourists were already streaming past eating gelato. Amy and Dio did not speak. They passed police officers at the doors of the Generalitat, walked through a metal detector, across a polished lobby, and down a long hall. It was an ancient building and smelled like furniture polish and dust. Amy opened a wooden door and they entered a brightly lit panelled room. Several rows of wooden chairs faced a small lectern. Beside the lectern was a wooden box, like a packing crate. Two men in business suits came forward and Amy introduced them, but Dio did not retain their names or titles. He was guided to a chair on the side of the room where, he was told, the *family* would sit. Amy sat on the other side, across a makeshift aisle. She smiled encouragingly, then leaned away to talk to one of the men in suits, their heads close together, whispering. Dio noticed another woman, seated beyond Amy. She wore a hat and had full lips, but Dio could make out – or at any rate later retained – little else. She did not look at Dio and he now looked down at his hands in his lap

---

18 The traditional seat of the Catalan government. It is a small but nevertheless imposing building, on a small but nevertheless imposing square. Only the oldest surviving seats of government in Europe and the Americas are able to pull off such paradoxically minimalist power displays. Later eras went for the monumental, and failed miserably.

and his feet on the floor.

Presently the door opened and Dio turned his head to watch three more women come in. They wore black, and were greeted by one of the men in suits who guided them to chairs behind Dio. One woman was very old and wore her grey hair pulled back in a tight bun. She looked severe. The other two were perhaps in their early fifties, and could have been sisters. They were tall and elegant. They glanced at Dio, then stared straight ahead with stern or vacant expressions.

They waited quietly. A fly made its way around the room.

At last one of the men in suits, after looking at his watch and once about the room, stood and approached the lectern. The other man glanced at Amy, who nodded, then rose and made sure the door was closed. After introducing himself (his first name, Vicente, was all Dio caught) and his association (Historical Memory), the man at the lectern began to speak, not surprisingly, about the past.

The past of forgetting is over, he said. The history of loss is closed. We know the way forward leads back, that our future is to be found by going through the door in the back of our history. The story of victims like Ramon Fernandez Hernan must be told – these stories *are* being told – and we are gathered here to receive them. The silence since Franco's death has left Spain with an underdeveloped historical memory. The movement to dispel this silence, to give voice to what has been without words, is a movement of grandsons and granddaughters. It is a movement of and for the future. But it begins in and with the past, in all its darkness and forgetting. It begins when we seize hold of a memory when it flashes up – when we grasp its image and do not let it go, but carry it before us like a torch into the night.

Vicente paused and the fly could be heard again. He held his hand in front of him, above the lectern, fist clenched, like he was indeed grabbing firm hold of something fleeting and fugitive. He was sounding much like Amy in her professorial mode. Dio noticed, for the first time, a slow-moving fan on the ceiling. Though the room was not overly hot, Vicente took a handkerchief from his pocket and dabbed his forehead. He was balding, a big man, yet not much older than Dio, with a florid face and a large, broad mouth. This was clearly an intense experience for him, even if only addressing a room with six people in it.

Brothers and sisters, he continued, Spain's remarkable modernization has only altered the surface of things. The important change, the change *inside*, is only just beginning. Many of the past's secrets have yet to be unearthed. For many, the recovery of the remains of a lost relative is only the beginning. We need to know circumstances and specifics. We need to know how and why. When we can unearth memory itself, in all its varied textures and colours, then we will have performed our task. But how can we describe this? It is liberation, plain and simple. Many in Spain have waited their whole lives for such a liberation, for their truths have been imprisoned long after the fall of the dictatorship. For many, such a liberation never comes. Today we give some flesh to bones, and forge a new way forward. Today, we must consider ourselves among the lucky and privileged.

Here Vicente gestured towards his small audience, holding his hands out wide, a smile frozen on his broad face. Dio glanced at Amy, who was listening to Vicente with rapt attention. He rather wished she looked a bit more sceptical.

My father, Vicente continued, is also among the victims. During the Franco regime, he and some dockworkers marched through the streets of Barcelona. It was the anniversary of the city's resistance to the coup. They marched in silence, without banners or signs or raised fists or songs. Slowly, like a funeral for democracy. It seemed even more defiant than barricades and overturned cars and hurled bricks. Many were arrested, my father among them. He was ten years in jail. But he came out alive. He was lucky.

Dio began to wonder about the women sitting behind him. He wondered about the woman beside Amy. He wondered where the fly had got to. Wondered how long all this would take. Vicente went on.

In the universe, there is matter and antimatter. This is what the physicists tell us – every particle has a mirror antiparticle with the opposite charge. When matter and antimatter meet, they annihilate each other. But what is strange, and what the scientists have not been able to adequately explain, is that, while there should, in theory, be as much antimatter as matter in the universe, there is, in fact, much much more matter. Practically everything that is, is matter. Aside from the void.[19]

Dio looked around quickly. No one looked as baffled as he felt.

Matter is winning this cosmic struggle, Vicente said, dabbing at his forehead, his voice rising dramatically. The scientists can't explain it, but matter is winning. We can take heart in this.

Dio looked at Amy again, and noticed the other woman glance at him, and smile. She had such a wise face. Not pretty, but complicated, noble. Proud even. How old was she? Maybe Dio's age, maybe older. Something mysterious happened when people

---

19   The science here is not exactly sound, as far as I know.

reached their forties. They seemed like they could be going in two directions at once – towards their youth, and towards their death. Sometimes a single glance conveyed both possibilities simultaneously.

To the family of Ramon Fernandez Hernan, Vicente was saying, the government of Spain expresses its sincerest condolences, and apologizes deeply for the crimes of past regimes. Even the dead will not be safe from this enemy if he wins. We will not let him win.

At this Vicente stepped back from the lectern, gathered himself for a moment, as though quite overcome, then looked up and, nodding his head, smiled reassuringly at his small audience, and took his seat again, once more dabbing at his forehead and neck with his handkerchief. After a moment Amy stood, her suit impeccable and her black hair carefully pinned back from her face, where a look of great concentration had taken hold. She approached the lectern, and looked down at the box by her side for a moment.

7

In another story, in another universe, written by another author, Dio and Amy make love in his hotel room. First they remove Amy's suit and blouse and panties. Then Dio's dusty clothes and his underwear with holes along the seams at his thighs. They lie on the bed, exploring each other, legs and arms entwined. Her warm skin. The almost imperceptible hair on her arms standing up. The scar on his hip. Amy rises up on top of Dio, and Dio stares past her breasts, past her cascading hair, at the ceiling above.

In the theory of alternate or multiple universes, because observations cannot be predicted absolutely, it is hypothesized that the range of possible observations corresponds to a range of different universes. Throw a die. There is a universe in which each of the six numbers comes up. Or, what does it mean to say that had Napoleon (or Hitler) not marched into Russia, his empire would not have fallen? Or more simply, if I hadn't ridden my bike down *this* street at *this* time, I would not have hit *that* pedestrian? It means, according to the theory, that there exists a universe in which Napoleon (or Hitler) in fact *did not* invade Russia and in which his empire *did not* fall as it did in our universe. It means there is a universe in which you *did not* ride your bike down this street, and you *did not* strike that pedestrian. Each decision we take spawns universes in our wake in which we in fact took other decisions.

In an alternate universe, the anarchist revolution in Catalonia was a success and prospers to this day. The fascists were defeated, and a stateless space for libertarian communism was declared and observed, allowed to fully develop and flourish. There is no private property and no money in circulation (capitalism is a word that refers to the arcane system employed in other parts of the world). Everyone has what he or she needs (modestly, of course), and everyone gives what he or she can (to the best of their various abilities). No one is exploited. All decisions are made at the local level, from the bottom-up, collectively. Energies that are elsewhere spent on accumulating wealth and consuming commodities or inventing new commodities to address invented needs are, in this Catalonia, put into the arts, the health and well-being of the population, and education. There are no forgotten mass graves. History is known intimately, locally, personally. It records the lives and efforts of even the most insignificant and forgettable. In this universe, documents of civilization are not mistakable for documents of barbarism. In this universe, Ramon Fernandez is a very old man whose poetry is known and memorized by many of his fellow citizens, a poet who can be found and approached, receiving strangers warmly at local cafés or along treed avenues. His books are readily available, for free, in the many open libraries. They have worn spines, and bear the faint pencil markings of many prior readers' annotations.

8

I will now tell you what we know about Ramon Fernandez Hernan, his life, and his death, Amy said, one hand gesturing towards the box beside her feet. For the first time Dio realized what was in the box: his great uncle's bones. Like some artifact ready to be shipped to a museum.

Ramon was born in Granada in 1897. The Fernandez family had only recently moved to the city, where his father, Emelio, opened a small, dry goods store. His mother, Mariana Hernan Piñeda, was a dark and quiet woman.[20] Little is known about the couple, other than the fact that they had come from the country. Ramon had a younger sister, Guadeloupe, born when he was two,[21] but the parents seem to have doted on their first born, sending him to a private school, which almost bankrupt the modest family. As a young man Ramon began to write poetry, and he befriended a circle of other would-be poets, including Federico Garcia Lorca, who would one day become so famous. Indeed, in 1919, Ra-

---

20 I am not entirely sure upon what research these details are based; I have myself seen no documents relating to Fernandez's parents that provides this sort of information.

21 The dating is difficult, as there are no records of Guadeloupe's exact birthdate. Fernandez himself, in a letter, refers to her as "his little sister, born when I was around two and beginning to walk more confidently into the world of objects and names." Even the exact date of Fernandez's own birth has been disputed. See, for instance, Pedro Balroyen's essay, "The Poetry of Andalusia, Birthplace of Spanish Modernism."

mon followed Lorca (or Lorca followed Ramon – it is not clear which[22]) to Madrid, where the younger poet was to study at the Residencia de estudiantes. Ramon, unable to afford tuition, lived nearby in the city, in the callé de Goya, working, perhaps as a waiter[23], and writing a great deal of poetry. At this point, many people were more impressed with Ramon's work than Lorca's, and they referred to Lorca as Ramon's imitator.[24] Ramon's poems were published in leading literary journals, and he was, in some small sense, the toast of Madrid's poetry cafés.

Dio listened carefully and with interest. What, he wondered, did being the *toast* of the town *in some small sense* mean? Surely, either one was, or one wasn't, the *toast*.

At this point, Amy continued, 1921 or 1922, things become difficult to track. Ramon ceased writing to his family in Granada. He does not appear to have published any more poetry. He split from Lorca and his circle. The Fernandez family does not hear from Ramon again until 1925. Tough times have befallen them, and like many Andalusians, they are contemplating the move north in search of work. It is then that Ramon writes from Barcelona, where he is working in a boot factory. Hearing that there is plenty of work in Barcelona, the Fernandez family decides to move to the city in 1926, but only after the death of Emelio Fernandez

---

22 The issue is compounded by a letter written by Lorca to Adriano del Valle in September of 1920, in which the poet writes, "I have gone through a crisis of distance and sorrows, brought about either by my following Ramon here, or his following me (you know the complexity of which I speak, having contemplated the blue sky too much, and having felt real wounds of light)." See *Federico Garcia Lorca: Selected Letters* (New Directions 1954).

23 The "perhaps" alone, here, is enough for us to sniff out the guesswork.

24 I believe this to be largely based on Manuel Altolaguirre's opinion, given in the introduction to the *Anthology of Spanish Romantic Poetry* (1933).

(from blood poisoning[25]). Mariana and Guadeloupe arrive in the city and find work as seamstresses. They see Ramon from time to time, but soon lose touch with him again.[26] Estrangements appeared to have dwelt at the heart of this family.

Here, Amy paused slightly, perhaps resisting the temptation to glance up quickly at Dio before continuing.

Soon Guadeloupe and her own mother have separated too, with Guadeloupe finding work in a dress shop, where she soon marries the head tailor. Before the war, it seems Mariana had moved back to Granada. It is not known what became of her there, but she does not seem to have survived the war years.

Here Amy paused again, shuffling some papers in front of her on the lectern. Dio had not noticed that she even had notes. She seemed to be drawing Ramon's story down from the ceiling, or up from the box of bones.

Our information about Ramon at this time comes from Luis Guillen, who worked with him in the Barcelona factory, served with him during the brief months they were active in the war, and later emigrated to Canada.[27] Luis's daughter responded to my email

---

25 Once again, I have seen no documents with specific family details like this. Of course, the Spanish government might have access to materials – or even first-hand interviews, I suppose – which I have not seen. If this is the case, I find it infuriating, having been turned aside by more than one archivist in Granada and Barcelona. When nationalism and scholarship collide, we all should shudder.

26 There is evidence that Fernandez visited Paris in the early 1930s, possibly in the company of anarchist exiles Durruti and Ascaso. See the introduction to my own "The Theatre of Criticism" in this volume.

27 Here I have to give thanks to Gloria Personne, for making me aware of this

questions from Toronto, noting that her father had spoken often of his dead comrade. In the factory, Ramon was known for his dedication to anarchist ideas and the CNT (the anarchist union). He was not known as a poet, not known to write any poetry at all, though Luis often saw him with papers, which he assumed

---

information, and for the efforts of Amy Godwin for her diligence in uncovering it. It is no exaggeration to call this *the* great leap forward in Fernandez scholarship. All my own work on Fernandez has been the direct result of this discovery; what I did not know before reading this text was the provenance of this material, now held in the CNT archive in Barcelona. For the reader's interest, and for comparison's sake, I append here my own brief biographical sketch of Fernandez, from the introduction to my translation of *The Quixote Variations* (BookThug 2008):

Ramon Fernandez was born in Andalusia, like many poets. He led a Spanish intellectual's and rebel's life not untypical of the early twentieth century. But he was more in the mold of Chilean Vicente Huidobro than other Spanish poets of his day (the Machados, Altolaguirres and Lorcas). There was an uninhibited wildness, it seems, a sense driving him not of a very old world with its rich traditions but of a very new one only just beginning to dawn. But we know very little about him, and he was, in almost every sense of the word, a 'minor' poet. The figure he cut amidst the Madrid literati was shadowy and fleeting; he left literary circles in the Spanish capital at some point in the mid-1920s, showing up on a factory floor in Barcelona (sewing leather boots). It is not clear whether he was abandoning his educated middle-class background or, as some have contended, merely a peasant/worker who by some miraculous ascension found himself amidst the ranks of the literati for a time, before returning to his forsaken class roots (like a Latin John Clare). However that may be, we know that in the Summer of 1936 he marched into Aragon in the Ascaso Column, an anarchist militia, and was never seen again. He comes down to us as the author of a few short ballads published (anonymously) in anarchist workers' newspapers (such as *Solidaridad Obrera*) and as the reputed author of one long poem, unpublished in full but well-known in manuscript: *Variaciónes del Quixote*. Little else is reliably known.

were anarchist tracts and copies of the anarchist newspaper, *Solidaridad Obrera*. When news of the fascist rising came, Ramon and others organized the boot factory workers immediately. Arms were distributed that very night, from a secret cache at the factory, and the workers took up positions just south of the Placa de Catalunya, on La Rambla. On July 19 1936 Ramon, Luis, and other workers from the factory fought the Spanish army – their own army – in the Placa, forcing them to retreat, and securing Barcelona for the anarchists, and for a free Spain. Ramon was injured, but Luis remembers them singing and dancing through the night, and riding cars up and down the streets the next morning, their guns held proudly, the cars painted in white letters with the names of the workers' unions and anarchist organizations – CNT, FAI – the black and red flags flying above them, horns honking. Then, at a gathering of boot factory workers, Ramon read a poem.

Dio thought of his little church and its pockmarked doorway. It was in *this* city, in *these* streets he had been walking these past few days, that all this happened. He looked across at the woman with the hat. She was bent over what appeared to be a notebook, scribbling quickly with a black pen.

Within days, columns of anarchist and socialist militias had been formed, and the march east, towards Aragon and the besieged city of Zaragosa, begun. Luis said that he often walked at Ramon's side, the older anarchist being something of a mentor and father figure, and the two would smoke and laugh and discuss the countryside or what anarchist communism would mean to all of their lives. (How will we get paid? We won't need pay – we will just get what we need. But who will provide it? Other workers, to the satisfaction of whose needs we will also contribute.) Ramon and Luis fought the fascists near Fraga, then found themselves driven back, dug in at a ravine near Alcarràs. Things went badly at Alcarràs, and the Barcelona anarchists were severely outgunned. Luis was injured and taken to Lleida. There he eventually met another worker from the boot factory, who told him that Ramon had gone missing and was presumed dead. This fellow had Ramon's small leather bag, which he had taken everywhere with him, and which contained a set of field glasses, a journal and a number of loose papers. These Luis asked for, and was given, and kept them his entire life, amongst his most prized possessions.

Amy shuffled papers again and took a deep breath, as though she herself was deeply affected by the proceedings.

I have here an email from Luis's daughter, Coleen. Luis is now over ninety years old, and suffering from dementia. But Coleen has always been curious about her father's past, asked him many questions, and wrote down everything her father could tell her about his Spanish years. She writes,

> My father liked to speak about Ramon more than anyone else – even his own parents and brothers. Luis and Ramon, it seems, were both the black sheep in their families – the radicals who talked revolution incessantly and disturbed calm dinner conversations with their exhortations and defiant critiques of the bourgeoisie. Ramon was some fifteen years older, so he took my father under his wing at the factory, and was even more watchful of him once the war began. Ramon taught my father everything he valued – that's what he said – and read to him from books that were in Russian and Italian, translating and explaining as he went. He taught him, as he often repeated to me, that the state of emergency we live in is not an exception but the rule. They never talked about poetry, so my father was deeply affected when he heard Ramon read a powerful poem at the victory celebration in the Placa de Catalunya, where

great crowds had gathered to hear Durruti speak. Then, after Ramon disappeared and my father claimed his small bag and its little archive, he was amazed to find even more poetry. My father liked to say, there is a hidden mystery in everyone, a silent language they speak only to themselves, and need no one else to hear. He saw this as the personal side of anarchism, the heart of its autonomous philosophy. And yet it was nothing without the love and solidarity one felt for one's comrades. My father said there were few men he would say or admit that he *loved*, but he loved Ramon, with all his heart, and with a passion that never cooled over his long life.[28]

Amy paused, moving papers once more. Dio felt a tingling along his scalp.

Nothing more is known of Ramon Fernandez's fate. Nothing until his remains were exhumed from a mass grave at that ravine

---

28 I can barely describe my feelings upon reading this. I allow the scholar to respond: if only we knew what poem Ramon read that day! Buenaventura Durruti was a leading figure amongst the Spanish anarchists and a driving force in the liberation and defense of a free Catalonia during the civil war. I quote here a famous passage from Durruti – one for which I can imagine Fernandez's poetic counterpart:

> We have always lived in slums and holes in the wall. We will know how to accommodate ourselves for a while. For, you must not forget, we also know how to build. It is we the workers who built these palaces and cities, here in Spain and in America, and everywhere. We, the workers, can build others to take their place, and better ones! We are not in the least afraid of ruins. We are going to inherit the earth, there is not the slightest doubt about that. The bourgeoisie might blast and ruin its own world before it leaves the stage of history. We carry a new world, here, in our hearts. That world is growing this minute.

near Alcarràs, after seventy years of mystery and doubt, this past July. There is evidence that Ramon was shot, probably a number of times, by rifle, but it is not known if he was shot during battle, and later buried, unidentified, in the mass grave, or if he was in fact captured by the fascists, and then shot by firing squad and dumped in the grave with his fellow captives. This we will never know. But we do know that Ramon was killed by Franco's army (the bullets used tell us that much), and that he died fighting for freedom, for equality and for solidarity. He is remembered here today by his nephew, Dioscoro Galindo, by his cousin Mateo Balan's daughter, Amaranta, and her daughters Arantxa and Dolores. Dioscoro and his father Ignacio, who is too sick to attend today's ceremony, proudly carry on their uncle's political work, as newspaper men and civil servants.

At this bit of absurdity, Dio felt himself blush.

Finally, at the request of Ignacio Galindo, I will read a passage from Ramon's 1920 poem, *Variations on the Quixote*.[29]

---

29 The reader may want to consult my own translation – the only English translation available – published by BookThug (2008). Here is a passage from my overview, from that book:

The material state of Fernandez's *modernista* masterpiece is the main problem. His few papers contain a jumble of handwritten verse passages, prose notes, and several drastically different typescripts of the poem entitled *Variaciónes del Quixote*, which redeploy material from the jumbled handwritten passages that accompany the drafts. The only prior translations – of a short seven-page section of the poem – by Edward Banderly (in *The Spanish Civil War in Literature: An International Bibliography*, edited by Peter Monteath, Greensward Press 1994) and in Stephen Collis's liberal misuse of the same material in *Anarchive* (New Star Books 2005) – are based on the *Litoral* fragment of 1920. But this fragment is substantially different from either longer typescript in Fernandez's papers; my suspicion is that the typescripts are later expansions of the

Amy paused, and held a piece of paper in her hands, staring at it intently. Then she began to read very slowly, with her eyes nearly shut. The words washed out at Dio with a strange foreignness he could not put his finger on. The words surrounded him and penetrated him. They were words, but he could not hear them so much as feel them striking some sort of silent bell within his body – all vibration and inner-storm. It was in part that his father – his father whom he never once heard even mention poetry, let alone read a poem, or remark that anyone he was related to was a poet – that his father *requested* a poem, *this* particular poem, to be read at his never once before mentioned uncle's funeral. So the words seemed to come all the way from South America, and to carry the weight of Aztec gold and cursed treasures with them – plunder of the new world, dark secrets of the old.

When Amy finished, she stood silently for a moment. Dio sat as though frozen by the words' ice and distance. He *felt* the poem more than he heard it, and it was as though something utterly alien had been revealed to him, then taken away, so that he had no chance to determine what it was he had just witnessed. Amy now smiled gently, nodded towards Dio and the others seated behind him, and then stepped away from the lectern. Doors on one side of the room, which Dio hadn't noticed before, were opened, and the two men in suits took up positions on either side of the doors. Dio could see a room with comfortable chairs through the doors, and a table set with coffee and perhaps some fruit and cakes. Amy beckoned Dio and the women to come, and they all silently repaired to the other room.

---

earlier version. Thus, for my translation I have more or less ignored the *Litoral* fragment (there is every indication that the anonymous piece was placed in the journal by Fernandez's friend Altolaguirre, without his consent or foreknowledge), relying instead on the longer typescript versions, cross-referencing them to arrive at as true and authoritative a draft as possible.

9

The small reception was one of awkward silences. Amy tried to say quiet things no one really seemed to hear. She gave Dio an envelope with an elaborate seal, touched his arm, and looked meaningfully into his eyes. She seemed to expect him to be overcome by grief, but it was only strangeness he felt, dislocation, light-headedness. Vicente and the other man stood by watching, idle and bored. Amy moved to speak to the woman in the hat, who stood to one side, holding her closed, black notebook. The three older women – distant relatives of Dio's that he had not even known existed – sat together and drank coffee and tried to disappear. Dio realized he should be saying something to them, but he could not fathom what. He kept thinking of the poem – a poem his father knew and asked for – and wondered why he had never been told about his great uncle's poems before. Or any poems for that matter.

He heard the woman in the hat speaking to Amy, her voice raised slightly in excitement. She was saying something about a painting, about some sort of painted figure with her face turned towards the past, where catastrophe and wreckage kept piling up. Dio imagined a highway collision of some sort. The woman spoke a strange Spanish – obviously not her native tongue. She occasionally used French words, even a few English ones, to get her meaning across to Amy. Dio liked the sound of her voice, which was almost musical, and the way she rolled forward on the balls of her feet as she spoke, her body straight and arms held slightly away from her sides, like a child who could not keep her body from dissolving into rhythmical movement. Or a dancer. He still could not guess her age – 30? 40? 50? This was not Dio's skill. Women occupied a world of their own he only knew by receiving the occasional audience, or reading government reports prepared by wooden civil servants like himself.

Dio shook himself into consciousness and approached the cousins. He nodded, and the two younger women nodded back. Awkwardly, he inquired after their health, and one of the daughters answered for the three. She in turn asked after Dio's father, and was told that he was very weak, and very old now. The old woman, Amaranta, snorted softly, and drank her coffee. The daughter who had spoken looked at her mother with narrowed eyes, then turned back and tried a small smile for Dio. She more or less succeeded. Then Amy came over to ask if they were happy with the ceremony. Too much ... bluster, Amaranta said quietly. But we thank you. Dio was embarrassed, and so was the daughter who had spoken to Dio. There was more silence while Amaranta finished her coffee. Someone commented on the weather, and then the drapes.

Amaranta stood, pulled a shawl about her shoulders, bowed her head in Amy's direction, barely glanced at Dio, and then walked in a dignified fashion towards the doors. Her daughters stood too, thanked Amy and Dio, made an excuse about having to get their mother home, and followed her out the door. Dio, still embarrassed and not wanting to look at Amy, looked down at a cup of coffee on the chair, still half-full, its dark liquid trembling.

*

The poem, Dio said to Amy.

Yes?

How did it ... where did you....

Amy smiled, a look something akin to delight on her face. It is part of a long poem which was published in a journal in Madrid in 1920. Probably Ramon's best-known work. At least, at the time, it caused something of a stir, it seems. Outrage and shock.

Dio frowned. But how did my father....

Amy continued to smile and nodded. Apparently he has always had a copy of the journal with your uncle's poem in it (which he got from your grandmother, the poet's sister), and has often read it. When he wrote that you would be coming in his place, he requested that this passage be read. I found a copy in the university archives. I am surprised he never spoke to you about it....

No, he never did. Dio paused. I'm surprised too. My father and poetry – those two things don't go together.

Amy and Dio were silent a moment. Then –

Did you like the poem, Amy asked?

Like it? *Like* it. I don't know.

Dio looked past the plate of untouched fruit toward a window. A yellow curtain moved, and the window, he noticed, was half-open. Vicente stood near it and watched the scene outside. He looked like he might jump through the window at any moment. Dio thought that would probably be a good idea.

Yes, I suppose I did like it. But ... I don't know poetry. It seemed ... to exist above, maybe even under, its own words, if that makes any sense. Like something was there, that was not there in the words. And it seemed to speak ... from where Ramon is now. Dead, I suppose.

Amy nodded. I think you do know poetry, she said.

It is strange though ... I don't understand it.

I don't think it's supposed to be understood very easily, if at all. Not the way we normally think of understanding things. And I think it is supposed to seem strange. To cast us out suddenly into a world we don't recognize, to have to learn all over again.

Dio noticed the envelope in his hands, as though for the first time. He held it up. Is this ... the poem?

No, a letter from the Spanish president.

Dio turned the envelope over distractedly in his hands.

I can hardly remember the words, he said, still thinking about the poem. What does it mean (and here Dio searched for the words) ... *I am a distant flame / and a sword far off* – ? How can one be a flame *and* a sword?

Amy shook her head. It's just what the poem says. What we do with it – Amy shrugged – that's up to us. Really, you should speak to Gloria. Amy and Dio both looked up, but the woman in the hat (this is who Amy seemed to be looking for) had left, perhaps when she saw the other women leave.

They were silent again. Then Dio remembered Luis.

Why did Ramon's friend go to Canada? I mean, I know why people left Spain after the war, but why Canada?

His daughter Coleen said it was a random choice, mainly inspired by the name of the Barcelona power company, which was called *El Canadiense*, because it was Canadian-owned – globalization, you know, before there was globalization. He said that a country that supplied power to the world must be a remarkable place – and a place filled with workers and factories. She said, instead, he found vast empty spaces. And powerlessness.

Dio nodded, again staring into an abandoned coffee cup nearby.

*

To their left, someone came hurriedly into the room. Looking up, Dio saw that it was one of the old woman's daughters. She smiled, embarrassed, and asked if she could talk to Dio. Amy excused herself, and Dio and his distant cousin sat down together.

She said her name was Arantxa, and she apologized for her mother's stern behaviour. She is old, Arantxa explained, and resents the past. Or wishes to forget it. She does not like being reminded of old things. Of what happened all those years ago. Or the bones under the ground. She was a child during the war you know. But I feel I must explain her a bit, and make an apology on her behalf.

Arantxa had a warm, inviting face. Her body was large but graceful. She was at least fifty, but Dio could tell she took care of herself. Her hair was black and fell in a perfect shoulder-length bob, falling in front of her face when she looked down, as she often did while talking. She wore a large silver ring on one of her strong-looking hands.

My mother knew your grandmother well. Visited her regularly. No one ever spoke about Ramon, except when there had been liquor, and then some of the men would talk, or Guadeloupe would. What I want you to know is that it was not only for his politics that Ramon was shunned or forgotten, but for his … sexuality.

His what, Dio asked?

86

His sexuality, that he was, at least rumoured to be, a homosexual. After the war, it was not good to have republicans in the family, near death to have anarchists. Your father was sent abroad out of this fear. But Guadeloupe was left alone. People, though, forgot the politics (or at least shoved it, temporarily, into a closet) and fell back upon other, time-worn hatreds, wounds, and embarrassments. Before the war, Ramon was the black sheep because everyone thought he was a homosexual. Never a wife, never a woman. That was an axiom in our family. First poetry, then politics. These were his passions, and he left one lover for the other. But no women were heard of. And then there was Lorca, his friend, who everyone knew was gay, and who Ramon followed to Madrid. So Ramon was guilty by association. Guilty of such a simple thing – loving a man instead of a woman – or maybe loving poetry, and then politics, more than any person, man or woman. I don't know.

Dio thought for a moment. He thought he could hear a clock ticking somewhere, but did not recall seeing one. He scratched his face, where a beard had started to grow.

Do *you* think he was a homosexual?

Does it matter? I don't know. Very likely I suppose. But it's no reason to bury him as deeply as this family did. My mother, even my sister, can't see that. All they see is Lorca the famous gay poet, and Ramon the infamous, or forgotten, mirror image. Most poets, you know, are not famous. Most are like Ramon – gone before you blink, with no one to recall their strange words. I'm glad we at least have his bones now. Something … solid. Material. Like a fact that can't be disputed.

Dio thought of the packing crate. Then he thought of the *Indiana Jones* movie, where the sacred object is placed in a crate, and the crate stowed away amongst thousands of other such crates in a giant warehouse, never to be found again. This movie had played, badly dubbed, for months in a theatre near Dio's home. He told Arantxa about this, but she did not know the movie.

It's American.

Oh.

They were silent a moment. Then Dio asked another question.

You said your mother visited my grandmother? You would have known her too…?

Yes of course. What a stoic woman. She had an iron will, built over a lifetime's hardship and loss. To think, losing both her husband and brother in the war, her mother wandering away to never be heard from again, and sending her only son away into exile. It's more than anyone should have to bear.

Here, Arantxa made vague gestures and shook her head.

Her husband, Dio asked?

The tailor, Enrique Covas. Strange, Guadeloupe's brother was killed by the fascists, but her husband was killed by the communists. By the time of the war, Enrique's dress shop had become fashionable and successful. He and Guadeloupe had developed bourgeois airs. They walked the avenues in the evening, arm in arm, well-dressed, of course. Enrique's brother was a priest, too, and in hiding (the churches had been attacked, burnt, priests chased out of towns or hung from their own bell towers, shot). Enrique's brother had betrayed several communists, early in the struggle, and they had been looking for him. They took Enrique into custody for questioning. That's what they said. This was almost a year after Ramon had gone missing. The tide was turning and the communists had replaced the anarchists in control of Catalonia. During the revolutionary period here in Barcelona, Enrique and Guadeloupe had put away their fancy clothes, adopting the garb and manners of the working classes. Even wearing the *mono*.[30] When the communists replaced the anarchists, such airs were no longer necessary. Still, the communists knew who Enrique was, and they arrested him, hoping to get to the brother. Enrique died in custody. No explanation was given. Tortured, no doubt. The priest was never found, but he turned up again after the war, proud of having foiled so many republicans and communists. He got his church back, under Franco. Served mass to men who had killed so many members of his *flock*. But Guadeloupe got nothing – former communists (now disguising their pasts) hated her as the wife of an informant priest's brother, while the victorious nationalists hated her as the brother of a fag anarchist.

But I never knew Guadeloupe to despair or give herself over to sorrow too much. I knew her from the early 1960s, when she was already an old woman, stooped and grey – old beyond her years, really. But strong, quiet, observant. Her eyes sparkled intelligently, and she would smile at us children, but said very little. My mother and sister and I would visit her, oh, once a week at least. She lived alone, in an apartment in one of the big buildings in the Eixample that had been divided up into units, on Calle de Bailen, near the

---

30 The overall worn by many working-class Spaniards. For a time in 1936, this became a symbol of the revolution. I note also, here, that the difference between those killed by the fascists and those killed by the communists is that the latter, as well as being the much smaller category, at least had their death's publicly acknowledged and mourned. Burial in the family plot makes certain differences.

Diagonal.[31] She had flowers on a small balcony, and little green parrots would sometimes roost in the plane trees she could see there on the avenue. We would come and clean up for her, and cook a Friday night meal. Fish or something like that. Eventually, my mother wanted to bring her to live with us, in Gracia. But she would not hear of it. Still, in the 1970s, she moved in with several other old women, in a big house one of them owned, near Girona, close to the sea. I can't remember the woman's name, but she was a very old friend, maybe even a relative of Enrique's. We saw her very infrequently then. Maybe only two times that we drove there in my father's car. Four old women living together in a big house, like it was some sort of retirement home. That's what I thought it was, but there was no staff, and my mother told me after that it was simply the old friend's house. That's where they all died, as we found out after.

Arantxa straightened her skirt in her lap, and took the coffee cup Amy offered her.

It seems the old women made some sort of pact. I don't know if that is true, but it's what the papers reported. They decided, apparently, to starve themselves to death. Suicide, but of a strange and horrible sort. So slow. Like a hunger strike. But a strike against what? They had plenty of money – at least the old woman who owned the house did. They could have had all the food they wanted. But they boarded themselves up inside. Nailed doors and windows shut. Stopped eating. And waited. They died slowly, one at a time, maybe the last one dying weeks after the first (this is what

---

31 Tourists typically prefer the medieval confines of the Barri Gotic, but personally, I have always admired the wide open modernist avenues of the Eixample. If this were Paris, the boulevards would have been built to prevent barricade building, but in Barcelona, they have more utopian origins. They are the original street art.

the paper said again). One was found in her bed, as though sleeping. Another in a chair in her room, surrounded by books, thin as a stick in her housecoat. The other two were found in the living room. One lay on a couch there – she died first, they think. The others just left her there. Her body was badly decomposed. Guadeloupe was dead in a chair nearby. She died, they said, weeks after the one on the couch. Imagine. What about the smell? And sitting there, waiting, while your friend decomposed nearby, in the stuffy, boarded-up house. Just sitting there, watching and waiting. What did she do? What did she think? It sounds like a story meant to frighten children, or turn sinners.

Arantxa shook her head and put her coffee down.

I used to picture something from time to time – I don't know if it was in the newspaper reports, or if I've only imagined it – but I would picture this. You'll think it strange. But I see a mixing bowl on the kitchen counter, with a wooden spoon sticking out of it. Just a plain bowl. Maybe one from my own childhood kitchen. Maybe it was there on my mother's counter when I heard about Guadeloupe's death for the first time? I don't know. But I used to see that bowl when I remembered the old woman's terrible end. Was it empty? Or dirty and waiting to be washed? Set out to bake something at the moment they decided otherwise and abandoned food? Or a reminder of what they were doing? I used to try so hard to understand something about that mixing bowl. So strange. It's probably some completely insignificant detail. But I used to focus on it so, convinced a great truth would be revealed to me if I concentrated hard enough.

Arantxa shrugged, and they were silent for a moment again before she continued.

I still think about her sometimes, shuffling around that dark house, weak, drifting in her memories, surrounded by dead friends, awaiting her own end, contemplating what becomes of the body, which she could see with her own eyes, smell with her nose. It's terrible. But as I said, she had an iron will. She chose this. And waited. And there was her son, thousands of miles away, alive but unseen for so many years, not knowing that his mother was killing herself like this. Choosing slow death, a gradual fading away – like the Sibyl, in the myth. Was she refusing the world, refusing any kind of future, just as she refused, or felt refused, by the past? Did she think of her son, who she hadn't seen in nearly forty years?

My father would have been in a hospital himself at the time, Dio offered. Somewhere about that time anyway.

Really?

Yes. Shot by soldiers.

Arantxa nodded, like this was obvious. So the trouble followed him too, halfway around the world. The men in this family are all Quixote's, tilting at ideological windmills.

What else was there to say? They drank coffee, and exchanged small pleasantries, which rang hollow. Eventually Arantxa rose to go.

My best to your father, Dioscoro. I did not know him of course, but Guadeloupe spoke of him sometimes. She was proud, I think, but worried that he was too political. That the fate of her husband and brother would follow him. Well-founded fears, it seems.

Dio held her large hand for a moment, then she was gone. Strange, Dio thought, Ignacio had so often been seen as political by other people, when he felt he didn't really have a political bone in his body. So it had always seemed to him at least, but maybe his sense of his father was clouded by thirty years of resentment in a wheelchair. What did his teenage father do during the war? Did he fight? Did he hide? It amazed Dio that he had never thought of this before. Then there was the poem, which Dio could not have imagined. And his desire to send his son back to the country he had fled and never returned to, to recover the remains of a forgotten uncle. And he recalled Amy's words – that denying having a political position was itself a political position. His sense of where things belonged, the map to which *he* belonged, was becoming more complicated every moment.

He suddenly felt very, very tired. Everything he'd heard and learned today swirled around him like an army of ghosts, chattering but barely audible. Like the dead, waiting for him to join them. Quiet voices he didn't want to hear anymore. He looked at Amy and said, I want to go.

10[32]

---

[32] It's at this point that we must, if we are to think of this as a complete text in any way, venture upon certain speculations. I have every reason to believe that a Chapter 10 was indeed drafted, but I have never seen a version of it, and can only surmise that the author suppressed it for unknown reasons. When I first received the draft, I immediately enquired (via email) about the absent chapter. I received no response. I fully intended to follow up again, but other issues arose, and, sadly, Gloria soon disappeared.

Clearly, Chapter 10 deals with the trip Amy and Dio take to Alcarràs, to visit the site of the mass grave where Ramon Fernandez's remains were found. I would expect that this part of the text would have contained descriptions of the drive and scenery; perhaps they would have taken Amy's car, a small

Opel (it might be a vehicle supplied by Historical Memory, with government identification on its side panels and a special license plate). They would have passed around the outskirts of Lleida on the A2; they would find Alcarràs to be a small town, a circle of stone buildings and narrow streets surrounded by farms. Just south of town, past some fields, they would find the site, along the steep and sandy banks of the Segre river, in a grove of cypress trees.

I can imagine a small scene here. Perhaps there would be now-wilting flowers left by the family members of the various dead – those who also had only recently come to terms with long-lost relatives. Some dedicatory poems, perhaps, pinned to the trunks of nearby trees, recalling to Amy, I would think, the scene from *Don Quixote* in the Sierra Morena and the verses of the pathetic Grisóstomo. She might have even quoted a passage from memory. It would no doubt be moving to be able to read what words were written there, or to hear what conversation occurred between Amy and Dio, her hypothetical recitation of the passage from Cervantes, the sincerity of her voice schooled in university literature classes, the way she touched Dio's arm or even held his hand for a moment, the feeling rippling through his body at her touch, electricity, people call that, metaphorically invoking the fleeting impulses of Eros and longing, or the feeling that accompanied them in the car while they drove across Catalonia, all diffuse light on dream-baked landscapes the only logical response to which was the surrealism of Dali. They might have grown precipitously close. Amy might have told Dio about her university years, still in her recent past, and her continuing friendships with some professors and students – activists, who were becoming increasingly indignant during these difficult economic times, plotting and planning things Amy would have to decide whether she, too, as a government employee no less, would get involved in or not. Perhaps she was worried about her job, and the stability of the Spanish government in the face of a shrinking economy. Would there still be money for Historical Memory? For digging up mass graves and holding ceremonies for the reclaimed dead? Perhaps she felt torn between the comforting and warm bureaucratic slowness of government and the speed of streets and actions, the rush of a crowd before a swarming police force.

Perhaps, as they stood together near the graves, a wind came up from the direction of the Segre, whirling dust up out of the ravine. Dio maybe turned to face it, his eyes squinting, letting the sand strike his face like the tiny needles of half-remembered lives. Amy might have stood, her head bent, her back to the wind, one hand on a pine tree's trunk, the other holding Dio's arm, her fingers tight around his wrist. There was something in that wind – something Dio couldn't place, but which seemed to be something more than a natural force – something sweeping up all politics and literature, ideas and lives lived, metal, fire, oaths, soliloquies – something of the unaccountable apparatus that seemed to hold them all in its grasp, seemed to hold all human history in its grasp.

I remind the reader again, though, that this is all pure speculation. An attempt to conjure something that is completely lost, but the absence of which beckons and fires the imagination. How badly we want completion! The tying together of loose ends. The reconciliation of accounts. We are rarely so lucky. All this footnote can really cover, responsibly, is some sense of the history of mass graves and their existence in modern Spain, to which I now turn.

Mass graves have, in fact, made their macabre appearance throughout history – and not just in moments of natural disaster, war and genocide. Take, for instance, the example of the *Cimetiere des Innocents* in Paris, in active use from the twelfth through eighteenth centuries. Situated beside the main market, just outside the city gates originally (though the city, of course, grew to surround and envelop the cemetery, which acquired walls), *Innocents*, the burial place of the poor and average, used mass graves – giant holes that lay open until filled, with thousands of bodies, at which point the hole would be covered and another opened. By the late eighteenth century *Innocents* was massively overcrowded and, after periods of heavy rain softened the soil and exposed remains, the smell was beyond tolerating. All the bodies were dug up and removed to the Paris catacombs – the abandoned mines beneath Montparnasse – the bones of some six million individuals, skulls stacked with skulls, femurs and fibulas stacked together like cordwood. Today, the shopping area of Les Halles, including its modern, sunken mall, covers the area where the bodies of *Innocents* used to moulder.

In contemporary Spain, the issue of mass graves has only recently been brought into the light of public discourse. The people of Spain have long known that mass graves existed in their various environs. Graves where republican, anarchist, and communist opponents of Franco were shot and dumped – both during the war and in the reprisals afterwards. How many? No one knows for sure. There was a "pact of forgetting" in Spain: during the Franco years, you could not mention these things, and then, in the return to democracy after Franco's death, it was seen as a threat to the fragilities of an open political system to speak of such past divisions and atrocities (much as certain misguided liberals find it "divisive" to raise issues of gender and race when the very viability of democracy seems in question). But in the recent decade – the first decade of this new century – something exceptional and unpredicted has happened in Spain: there has been an upsurge of interest in and discussions about the country's troubled past, and a desire to recover and reconcile its losses. Not without argument, not without disagreement. But a new generation no longer wishes to forget, or so it seems. Now, some 2,000 unmarked grave sites have been identified, sites which possibly contain the bodies of more than 100,000 missing opponents of Franco. Many of these sites are being opened now by teams of archaeologists and forensic experts, working under the direction of the Association for Historical Memory. Families are finally finding and burying their dead.

How are the graves found? It is the memories of the elderly that must be relied upon – people who, as children, heard the stories or saw the atrocities or the evidence of their aftermath. The only archive available is one of flesh and blood, neurons and synapses – the most fragile of all archives. One woman, now in her eighties, remembers walking along a road near her village, in 1937, and seeing blood seep from the ground by the roadside, where until recently a ditch had lain. She led the archaeologists to the exact spot, some seventy years later. The ground was broken, and the bones laid bare. Stories like this are common and often provide surprisingly accurate information.

Of course the most famous of these unmarked graves is that of Lorca, whose remains, despite recent attempts to locate them at long-suspected sites, have proved fugitive. Perhaps no one really wants to find that grave. Perhaps it is all the more potent in its being lost, unmarked, forever hidden from us. But as the reader of this text now knows, Lorca is not the only poet to meet such a fate, and the pattern of anonymity is far more common. The famous may not be found, but the common and completely forgotten may be. And this is heartening somehow, for all of us "minor figures" in history. The grand and celebrated can survive their being unlocatable – myth and legend are their very lifeblood. But those who are already anonymous cannot long suffer this further elision.

I conclude this long, too long footnote, with a quotation from another victim of history – the German (Jewish) philosopher Walter Benjamin, who died on the Spanish frontier in 1939, trying to escape France and another fascist

The drive back to Barcelona was strange, though uneventful. The lights of Lleida came and passed quickly, but then it was mostly darkness, the sun having begun to set even as they had left the lonely hillside near Alcarràs. Dio may have slept for a while. If he did, what transpired in his mind was as much a day- as a night-dream, and was more or less a replaying of the day's events, with odd appearances by his father and Leandro's wife's illness. Throughout there was the pervasive sense that something deeply, enigmatically significant had occurred – something from which Dio would never fully recover – but something, equally, he would never be able to name or explain or tell anyone about. It was in the simple details of what had transpired. It was buried in subtlety and nuance. There, beside the open ground of Spain. Meanwhile the Opel Corsa hurled along the highway. He and Amy rarely

---

machine eager to fill mass graves. Benjamin here offers the caution we must heed: the same thinking that produces fascism will not successfully oppose fascism.

The themes which monastic discipline assigned to friars for meditation were designed to turn them away from the world and its affairs.
The thoughts which we are developing here originate from similar considerations. At a moment when the politicians in whom the opponents of Fascism had placed their hopes are prostrate and confirm their defeat by betraying their own cause, these observations are intended to disentangle the political worldlings from the snares in which the traitors have entrapped them. Our consideration proceeds from the insight that the politicians' stubborn faith in progress, their confidence in their 'mass basis', and, finally, their servile integration in an uncontrollable apparatus have been three aspects of the same thing. It seeks to convey an idea of the high price our accustomed thinking will have to pay for a conception of history that avoids any complicity with the thinking to which these politicians continue to adhere.

spoke. There was a look of peace and satisfaction on her face as she followed the road in the night. Like she had been through something entirely pleasurable, and could now drift above the warmth of its glowing embers. She may have spoken for a while – about her childhood, what she loved about Spain and old Spanish men, about lovers and university – Dio wasn't sure, as he drifted, looking into the Catalonian night. What vacuums lay beyond the visible here, what trains crawled slowly and unseen through this night? What cargo were they carrying, and where did it come from? Was the way to Montserrat lying there? A gorge down a dusty side road where you could go rafting? Some caves nearby where bandits used to hole up – all the way back to Roman times? Perhaps even further, into the depth of prehistory, all bones and drying pigment? A dog, perhaps, sat right on the edge of the freeway, as though it was just casually watching the lights of cars roar past at 140 kilometres an hour? A wild or cartoon dog without principles or concerns?

Barcelona eventually came up quick and bright, like light striking a silver gun barrel in the dark. As they came along the Via Laietana, Dio asked to be let out a few blocks from his hotel, so he could walk and clear his head. Amy held his hand a moment, looked intently into his face, and then reminded him to take the little red book with the repeated series of images running down the right-hand side of its cover – two men on horseback, one with a lance held in his arms.

On his way to the hotel, Dio stopped at a small shop on the cathedral square and bought some wine. The shop clerk was, Dio thought, Muslim, but he wasn't sure Muslim's were allowed to sell alcohol. Or were they only forbidden from drinking it? He pondered this while digging in his pocket for euros.

Back in his room he opened the wine (he had to borrow a corkscrew from the front desk, which did not seem to amuse the old clerk) and poured a large glass (in the water glass from his bathroom, where he had to remove its small, paper cap). It was good – not as good, he thought, as some of the wine from his Chile (this, he realized, was an unfounded boast) – but good, for such a cheap bottle. He'd chosen something local, from Tarragona. After draining the first glass, he poured another.

What else to do? Everything seemed so … immaterial, for such a distance he'd travelled – shouldn't he hold his ancestor's bones in his arms and rock them back and forth? Shouldn't he have fallen on the earth of the grave and scratched and pounded at the ground? Shouldn't he throw a brick through the window of … of … what? Where is the window he can shatter that displays the office of all of time's persecutors and murderers? They say history is written by its victors; surely they must have a sign out on some street somewhere, have ads in the papers? Dio was sure he'd seen them, in fact. Their logos were plastered over much of the world.

Dio laughed at himself, and drained his glass. He poured another, stood and did a little dance, and laughed at himself again. In the bathroom, he stared at himself in the mirror. Lines, hair graying slightly at the temples, thinning on top. Not handsome, just plain. Face like a cartoon – a sketch that needs filling in. A bit of the kicked dog about him (somewhere in the eyes or chin perhaps). A doormat. Lapdog. He stuck his tongue out, then gave himself the finger.

What the fuck was the Department of Historical Memory anyway? What were they actually accomplishing? Dio would rather have seen Amy in army fatigues and a beret, with a gun slung over one shoulder. They should be tracking down the real killers, met-ing out real justice. None of this ceremony bullshit. How much money was spent on fancy words, on flights and hotels, on putting on a good show? Historical Memory made Dio think of science fiction (a strange paradox he only half-acknowledged) – of secret underground catacombs filled with archives and time-travelling agents in search of the roots of future disasters and plagues, future uprisings and utopias. Dio poured himself another glass of wine, at once angry and amused by these thoughts.

He turned on the television and began to surf through the channels. The usual problems met his eye: footage of a large ship on fire, smoke billowing from its superstructure; protesters filling some darkened street, clashing with police in full riot gear, batons swinging and canisters of tear gas arcing through the night; a celebrity in tears. Then the commercials. A facial cream (the woman in the commercial spreads it on her face with a look of complete ecstasy). A car hugs a curving road, popular music blaring. A public service announcement about racism and immigration (showing a group of Muslim children playing with a ball in an ancient-looking street).

Finally Dio found the same talk show he'd seen part of the other day – the one in which the smoking man talked to two beautiful women. This time his guest was a rather weathered-looking fellow that Dio recognized instantly as a South American Indian. They spoke a mixture of Portuguese, Spanish and Catalan, with the interviewer often translating the Indian's Portuguese (when they weren't speaking Spanish) into Catalan. Dio managed to follow along, though. The Indian represented a group – a movement it seemed – of landless workers in Brazil who were involved in land reform activism. The Brazilian constitution, apparently, had a clause about the social use of land, and the Indian's movement would occupy land that it deemed was not being used to its full *social potential.* A court battle would ensue between the landowners and the squatters, with the squatters often coming out on top because of the constitution. The Indian spoke of threats and violence. He spoke of road blockades and shootings – *massacres*, Dio was pretty sure he said (the interviewer repeated the word several times to be sure). The interviewer, for his part, often asked inane and rude questions, like whether the Indian owned any valuables or personal items he was particularly fond of, and what they were, and where he kept them. Or whether his wife knew what he was up to, and whether she approved, and where he planned to raise any children he may now have or could expect to have some day. The Indian managed to ignore the most obnoxious questions, turning instead to issues such as the structure of the organization (it was grassroots, with every decision made, if possible, at the local level, by the groups of squatters, known as *nucleo de base*). The interviewer noted that someone called Fourier had foreseen a future in which four moons would illuminate the earthly night, ice would recede from the poles, and the oceans would be made of lemonade, and inquired as to the activist's opinion. The Indian said he wasn't sure about the lemonade or moons, but that he believed the polar ice was indeed receding. He'd read about it on the Internet.

After a commercial, the show returned without the Indian, he being replaced now with the two beautiful women Dio had seen the other day. The host and the women carried on a seemingly rollicking conversation, complete with laugh-track and obscene gestures (one of the women more or less lifting her short skirt and bending over in front of the camera, revealing a red thong), all in a fast-paced Catalan that Dio couldn't really follow. They smoked and laughed, and Dio watched a while longer, becoming both disinterested and vaguely offended. He wished the television had real porn on it rather than this shit, but he'd already checked for pay channels and there weren't any.

What would it be like, Dio wondered, to step seamlessly into another language? To be able, without training or the labour of learning and practice, to instantly be able to function fully in a foreign language – to understand and speak it at the drop of a hat? To understand the particular history and knowledge that came with it – the way of conceiving the world and one's relation to it? That would be a formidable power, one Dio wished he had. He'd speak the Indian's language. They could discuss land reform and polar ice, smoking together and talking long into a South American night.

His mind began to wander. He slept for a while. Then he awoke, remembering something that had happened with his father many years ago.

12

Once, when Dio had just begun his work for the city, and was living on his own for the first time, he received a strange phone call from his father. Strange, in part, because Ignacio never called. In fact, he never seemed to use the phone at all. Dio could not remember ever having spoken to his father on the phone, though surely he must have. Ignacio simply said, Come over, I need help with something. Asking for help was also something Ignacio did not do. What, asked Dio? He looked at his dishes piled in the sink. The smoggy view from his balcony. Come over, Ignacio said, I want you to help me.

Dio put on sweatpants, found his keys, took his bike off the balcony, and headed out. The ride was only a few kilometres ride, mostly downhill, though some of the roads were dirt in the low area near the shantytown. Great white-and-black clouds stood piled on the mountains to the south. But otherwise it was nice – not too hot yet. Spring, like it was now in Barcelona.

To ride in La Ciudad, you had to look at the road – the ground itself – directly in front of you at all times. There was no other choice, the roads were so poor. Potholes, broken asphalt and concrete, deep ruts in the dirt – you could be thrown down at any time. Cars and pedestrians didn't matter (they were mostly beyond Dio's control). Trucks would roar beside him, and he had to hope they were watching him in their mirrors. The ground he could not take his eyes off of.

Rut.
Hole.
Open sewer.
Car battery.
Massive crack.

Dio would call these sights out in his mind, concentrating. As though he had to name each object, reciting them like a mantra as he narrowly avoided them.

Cinder block.
Hole.
Really big hole.
Dead rat (big enough to dump his bike).
Alarm clock (looking like someone shot it).
Rut.
Sewer.

Dio took his bike – a ten-speed he worked on relentlessly, tearing it down, cleaning, replacing worn parts – around back of Ignacio's small house, one he'd moved to only a year or so ago, when Dio left – a ground-level place with a ramp entrance from its last, similarly wheelchair-bound inhabitant. He went right in, opening the back door and calling for his father at once. Ignacio answered from the living room and Dio went in, noting some stray books on a table in the hall, a broken umbrella lying hopelessly on the floor, and the general disarray of the place (which was no better or worse than Dio's apartment).

Ignacio sat in his wheelchair, his television improbably cradled on his lap. Dio looked at him for a minute, the old man staring back blankly, like a thief caught in the act, craning his neck to peer around the large, brown box.

What's going on?

We're taking this somewhere, Ignacio answered, indicating the television. It was pretty big, and Dio wondered how the old man got it onto his lap (he could barely see him behind it). He ran his hand over the back of his neck.

Is it broken?

No.

Where are we taking it?

To a friend.

You want me to take it there for you?

No. You push. Ignacio gestured behind his wheelchair. Dio stood there, looking at his father, Ignacio staring back impassively.

Is it far, Dio asked? I have to do some shit later (he was thinking of his new girlfriend, Malinche, who frightened and excited him).

Ignacio stared at his son. Maybe he was getting mad, it was hard to tell. Then he said, calmly, Yes, it's far. But I need your help. Push me.

So there was nothing else to it. With a sigh, Dio moved over behind the wheelchair, took the foam grips in his hands, one of which was badly split and showed the remains of past attempts to tape it back together, and began steering towards the door. It was difficult to get the chair started in the thick carpet. He leaned back, arms extended, head down.

You OK with that on your lap, Dio grunted?

Fine, Ignacio said, his hands on either side of the television. It wasn't small either, barely fitting on the old man's lap, its top covered in dust, its fake-wood sides dull, its screen grey and blank, the cord trailing behind so Dio had to pick it up to avoid tripping, wrapping it around one of the wheelchair's handles.

Down the ramp out front and into the street they rolled. Left, said Ignacio. There was no sidewalk so they had to go in the road. Nice day, said Ignacio, looking up at the blue sky and the white clouds piled high on the mountains ahead. He sounded like someone who had just climbed into a cab. Dio grunted, pushing up the slight incline. There were few cars on the road, though some kids went by on bikes, talking rapidly to each other. Ignacio told Dio to turn left at the next corner.

They rolled along for blocks. Past small bungalows, past a strip of mostly vacant shops with faded signs and past empty paved lots where the asphalt buckled and cracked. Presently they passed some tall, concrete apartment towers that had been crumbling since they were built in the 1970s. On the other side of the towers was the shantytown, filling a great gulley the grey apartment towers overlooked, almost tipping over on the poor masses huddled below. Down Dio and Ignacio went, the road little more than a dirt track here, stagnant water in a ditch at its side. Dio had a difficult time now, holding the chair back rather than pushing as they bumped down the hill. His back and arms hurt. Ignacio had to be uncomfortable too, clutching the heavy television, which practically bounced in his lap.

They passed a dead animal – a tapir or a pig.

At the bottom of the gulley, the freeway passed close and the path they were on was practically on its shoulder. Trucks and cars hurtled past. Dust and garbage – an old chip bag maybe – flicked up into the air, swirling. Ignacio told Dio to steer down off the side of the freeway, into the shantytown, then back under the freeway as it rose up on concrete posts to curve and lift out of the gulley. They passed corrugated tin shacks and cardboard lean-tos. People stared but hardly seemed surprised by the old man in the wheelchair with his television. A dog barked. Dio was sweating, exhausted really, a little embarrassed perhaps, and becoming angry. They had covered several kilometres, taking up the better part of an hour. Dio's feet and calves hurt and his hands burned. What was the old man up to? All he did was sit in his living room and watch this damn television. Now, out of the blue, they were rolling halfway across La Ciudad with it. He seriously considered that the old man had gone well-and-truly insane.

It was starting to rain.

They turned away from the shacks and under the freeway. There, in the shadows, Dio could just make out some packing crates and other rubbish – shacks and lean-tos even more miserable and ephemeral than those they had already passed. Some figures were hunched over a small fire. Ignacio pointed towards them. There, he said, take me over there.

Dio pushed the pitching and lurching wheelchair across the uneven ground, grunting. At the fire, three or four men stood and watched them. One came forward, smiling, and immediately took the television out of Ignacio's hands without a word. The old man rubbed his thighs, but Dio wasn't sure they felt any pain, or anything else for that matter. He was too tired himself to care anyway. The man who took the television put it on the ground and admired it for a moment, before turning back to Ignacio and speaking to him. Dio did and did not understand what the man was saying at first. Then he realized it was Portuguese. The men were Brazilians, black, hungry but with intense and smiling faces. Ignacio spoke to them in their language, which impressed Dio, who only understood the words that were the same or similar in Spanish. Still, he barely paid attention, as he'd begun to think about Malinche and leaving as soon as they could. Ignacio introduced Dio (as, Dio seemed to recall, *a spoiled loafer in the garden of knowledge*, or some such epithet), and Dio shook hands with the ragged-looking men.

One of the Brazilian men asked if Ignacio still drew cartoons. The old man said no, and the Brazilian asked him why not. There was a long silence while Ignacio appeared to consider this. Dio considered it too. Why hadn't he ever asked his father this question? Ignacio finally said, with a dismissive wave of his hand, it's all a cartoon now anyway, so what's the point? You wouldn't even notice the joke.

They spoke awhile longer, about things Dio mostly didn't understand, but which didn't seem very significant, then Ignacio suddenly said, Let's go. With a shrug Dio took hold of the chair again and pulled his father back towards the light, out from under the freeway. The Brazilians waved and turned back to the fire. One of them sat down on the television, and the others laughed.

The rain had stopped, or at least slowed. As they began to retrace their path, a dog made a great racket in the shantytown. It sounded like someone was killing it, and they could just see its legs and tail writhing in the dust behind a shack, before being pulled out of sight and silenced.

They went on along the freeway. After a few minutes, Dio asked who the men were. Peasants, Ignacio said, men without land or home, who have had to leave their own country because of expropriation and persecution. Exiles. I knew one of them when I ran the paper, the first time he came from Brazil to talk to the homeless here in La Ciudad.

Dio thought for a moment. Then asked what the men were going to do with the television. Ignacio made a vague gesture, like the question was irrelevant.

They needed it, he said, for their work. That's all. I wanted to help them.

Plus I watch too much TV, he added after a moment.

Plus, he said after another pause, Amelita says her brother has a new, better one for us. Colour.

They climbed the hill out of the gulley and past the apartment towers that impinged upon this low, weary place. Above the towers were the clouds that they had seen earlier over the mountains, like someone had stacked them on top of the concrete blocks of the apartments, to make the world outside the gulley even higher and harder to attain. Dio toiled behind his father's chair, past the dead tapir or whatever it was, thinking of Malinche and how angry she was going to be that Dio had not called yet, and how her dark hair fell about her, and the way she read a book, or even the paper, with alternately angry and laughing eyes, somehow managing to talk at the same time as she was reading, conversing with the paper like it was an able opponent with sometimes similar, but often opposite, views. Like it was someone urgently in need of her opinions.

13

Dio's clock radio came on at 7:00 AM Barcelona-time, volume loud, without his remembering having set the alarm in the first place.

First Voice: – of the concept of such a progression must be the basis of any criticism of the concept of progression itself.

Second Voice: Ok. You've lost me a bit there. Can we go back to the Trotsky story?

First Voice: Sure. It goes something like this. Some bandits broke into the house in Mexico City where Trotsky was killed.[33] I guess it's kind of a museum now. Anyway, they broke into his mausoleum and stole his ashes! The article says the ashes were in *a large silver vase inscribed with his name,* and the vase had his red scarf wrapped around it. They took the ashes and replaced the vase

---

33 Leon Trotsky was assassinated in his home in Mexico City on August 20, 1940, by N K V D agent Ramon Mercader, an ice pick blow dealt to his head while reading. The house was indeed converted into a museum; about the rest of the details here I am not able to comment.

with another one that looked just like it, then locked up and fled into the night. The only reason anyone knows anything about it is that the paper in Mexico City – other papers too, but this article comes from Mexico City – received this letter from the bandits that *told* them what they'd done. The letter also came with a small package of cookies.

Second Voice: Cookies.

First Voice: Yeah, cookies. Now are you ready for it? The bandits had *baked Trotsky's ashes into the cookies!*

[Both voices – perhaps a third too – laughing]

Second Voice [incredulous]: They baked him into cookies!

First Voice: That's right.

[More laughter.]

Second Voice: I'm sorry. I know it's really horrible, and there you are with your uncle's ashes – but to make cookies of someone's remains! I can't help laughing.

First Voice: It says (the letter from the bandits), *they are a little sandy, but delicious!*

[More laughter. Some one coughing]

Second Voice: Does the article say why the bandits did it, or who they were?

First Voice: No, it just calls them bandits. But it does say something about the date – it marks an anniversary, of ... ah, *the suppression of the Kr-onstad-t uprising.* Ah, yeah. Kron-stad. So I think you're right – they probably were anarchists after all!

Second Voice: Why was Trotsky in Mexico? He was a Russian, right?

First Voice: I think so.

Second Voice: So why Mexico? Better cookies?

[Laughing again]

First Voice: I don't remember ... he was in exile anyway, on the run from Stalin I guess. Presuming that's who had him killed. This was back in ... 1939 or something. But here's what I wanted to get to, to come back around to the topic of progress. The article says, quoting the bandits, *that history does not begin and end with the past – a small group of bandits can still give new direction to fights thought long to be frozen in time. Time itself is not homogenous and empty, but filled with struggles that break and flake off anew.*

Second Voice: What the hell does –

14

Dio slammed his hand down on the radio beside his bed, silencing the chattering voices. He rolled over and stared up at the ceiling. It's going to come down, he thought. It will crush me in this bed.

Amy called a few minutes later. She would pick Dio up in an hour, for the interment on Montjuic. Then, she suggested, they could go for a bike ride. This may have been a little insensitive, but it suited Dio well enough. After checking the time again, he called home. Malinche was on her way out the door, something about a late meeting with the tribal council about work on the new mine at Altoto, the damage dynamiting was doing to houses and, especially, the potential pollution of the river, and the unilateral (that's what she said, *unilateral*) way the corporation was making these decisions, completely without anyone's consent (especially the indigenous people that had been living there for, what – forever!). Everything's fine though, Dio. Maria is here to babysit. And the girls are too busy to even notice you've been gone for a few days. Plus we talked just last night!

Dio was surprised – he didn't remember at first, but then it dawned on him. The only thing was, he remembered none of the details of their conversation! And he certainly didn't remember anything about Malinche attending council meetings or being concerned about mines. Let's get off the line, she said, we can't afford this!

Dio thought about his kids. He thought of bikes and kids and accidents. He thought of how ridiculous it was to even think of riding a bike in La Ciudad, and yet he did, and insisted his kids did too. They were doing OK by La Ciudad standards, really, but still they rented an apartment, had no car, had to be careful with money. They weren't of La Ciudad's new and shining ruling-class, which seemed to have appeared as suddenly as the bright new shops and bars they frequented, nor were they living in the city's expansive shantytowns; they were in some barely existing and downwardly mobile middle ground. Dio worried about the government cancelling the ridiculous program that provided him with his pointless job. Worried about accidents befalling his kids, his wife maybe leaving him (was there any basis for this?), his father finally dying, as if the thirty years of his infirmity has been one long, arduous deathbed scene.

Did Dio even know his daughters? His wife? What they thought about when not really doing anything at all? And what had he done? Thrown whatever he'd been given around like it was worthless. Paid no real attention. Been too afraid to stick his neck out in any way. Always seemed like he was waiting for something to come along and make things mean something. And now he needed to pee all the time, because he was getting older and should have a doctor put his finger up his ass and check his prostrate. There were other things to worry about too. Poverty. The changing climate. What could he do? Cushion the blow, he thought, cushion the blow. But how? How does anyone do anything?

He showered, dressed, and went down to the lobby for his coffee and croissant.

The ceremony was simple. Only Dio, Amy and Vicente attended. The crate from the other day was replaced by a small, well-made and darkly varnished (or painted) box, which was inserted into a wall of niches on the side of the mountain by an official of the cemetery. Some of the niches had glass fronts – little windows on the afterlife – which Dio found humorous and strange. Like televisions, he thought, with one sad and eternal show playing. No more formal words were spoken, or if they were, they were of little substance and not very memorable. Vicente, Dio noticed, gave Amy a knowing look – almost a wink – touched her arm, his hand lingering there, and then left while Amy and Dio walked for a time amongst the graveyard's paths on the mountain. Amy pointed out the graves of famous anarchists and socialists and poets and Dio nodded absently. The sky was a perfect blue, but it was cooler than the day before.

This is it then, Dio thought. The end of my story here in Barcelona. The end of Ramon's. *Closure* was the word people sometimes used – whatever that meant. There was simply no longer any reason to be here. Dio looked at Amy. She was smart and young and beautiful and entirely foreign and strange to him. What else could possibly transpire between them? What was left for Dio to do? Just a return flight home, the return to his regular life and routines. Nothing more to tell about this unexpected episode in his life.

Dio remembered Luis in Canada, who would die many thousands of kilometres from here. He wondered about the email from his daughter too. And Ramon's journal. Was it really true that this old man had spoken so often of Dio's great uncle? He asked Amy if it didn't seem a little strange, even hard to believe. She simply replied that all stories are at bottom strange – even the ordinary ones. Dio didn't exactly know what this meant, but sensed something oddly defensive, or evasive, in Amy's manner.

A bus took them back down to the city, and they quickly found a rack of the *Bicing* bicycles, which Amy rented with a card she had in her bag. And so they set off along the broad streets of the Eixample. The bikes were a bit clunkier than Dio was used to, but the streets were wide and smooth, Amy was a good rider, and Dio found the pace of keeping up with her comfortable – not too fast, not too slow. They passed big turn-of-the century apartments, the university, and crossed the Placa de Catalunya, scattering pigeons. They stopped for a moment and Amy pointed out the Telefonica, the old telephone company building which the anarchists had seized in the early days of the struggle. Your uncle, she told Dio, would have run through those doors, a gun in his hand. Dio looked, half-expecting to see a group of bandits storming the building at that very moment. It was, in fact, entirely covered with white plastic, like a building-sized bag, another renovation project.

They rode on, down La Rambla towards the water and the tall column with Columbus's statue on top. There were many cabs here, and tourists everywhere, so talking was difficult. Dio mostly rode behind Amy, watching her calves work the pedals, day-dreaming a bit, entertaining the stray and not very serious erotic thoughts that play through the mind, and smiling at Amy once in a while when she looked back at him to point to a building (one had umbrellas sticking out of its side and a dragon leaping out over the street, like the bowsprit on a boat) or something funny (a tourist struggling with a huge birdcage). He thought about the spokes of wheels and how they sometimes appeared to be going backwards. Why was that?[34]

A kid ran across the road and Dio swerved. Lucky. Amy looked back and yelled something, but kept riding.

Dio thought of his family again and their daily lives and trips to the market or riding his bike to work on broken roads. He momentarily entertained the not-uncommon fantasy of never returning home, of shedding his past life like a skin, of beginning anew in a new world with new possibilities. He laughed at this. He was far too unadventurous, he knew. Plus he could not imagine not seeing Malinche and his girls again, and being immersed in the familiarity of their daily routines. Not empty time but time filled with the presence of now and the everyday. Of immediacies and the moments one passed through, one to the next, following the unfolding of life like a string through a forest.

---

34 This is more common when a wheel is seen turning on film. I remember, as a child, being mesmerized by the turning wheels of a stagecoach in some old western film. The result is sometimes the subconscious sense that we must be moving backwards in time, "turning the clock back" as it were.

At the bottom of La Rambla, where there is a roundabout, they circled the column. Dio wondered why it was there – did Columbus sail from here? Wasn't it … Seville? Cars came from all angles and Dio was a bit nervous – he'd been hit before, more than once. He watched a truck come straight at him and pass so close its draft alone almost caused him to lose control. Its side was painted with a large advertisement for something called *Jetztzeit* – a German product, he assumed. When he looked for Amy again he couldn't see her. He looked all around, coasting, then spotted a woman on a *Bicing* bike, some distance away, heading along the waterfront away from the column circle. He set off after her, peddling hard.

Down they sped towards the beaches, through Barcelonita. Dio caught her after a couple of blocks, but it wasn't Amy – he could tell that when he came within a half-block of her. In fact, if you could have observed Amy and Dio riding from above, maybe from the top of the column, resting like a tired and stranded angel with one arm around Columbus and leaning out over the scene below, you would have seen them trace two diverging lines, as Amy left the circle in one direction, back towards the city centre, and Dio, shortly thereafter, in another (towards the beaches) – like separate planetary bodies speeding off into opposite and potentially limitless reaches of space – satellites using a planet's gravity to sling themselves towards divergent and unknown cosmic destinations. He slowed, looking around, gliding towards the beach, wondering where she had gone. Did she have a cell phone? It didn't matter, Dio didn't, and he didn't know her number anyway.

He should circle back, return to the column, but for some reason he coasted on, looking around, sinking into the sense of being lost – into the reassuring arms of fate and the inevitable, into a complete lack of will or responsibility. Not that he couldn't figure out where he was, or the way back, but that other people didn't know where he was, and this for some reason began to feel comforting. Like he was well-hidden. Anonymous. And he realized that above all, he was beginning to want to hide. To disappear into the thick fabric of the present, where neither past nor future could tug his sleeve or hold tight to his leg.

15

Dio only remembered later – was it during the ceremony? Did he fall asleep in the warm room at the Generalitat? Or in the car while Amy drove to Alcarràs? No. It must have been the ceremony, maybe on Montjuic. Maybe a dream. Maybe something actually said, but altered in remembrance. Dio half-awake or asleep but still just hovering on the edge of consciousness where sometimes the strangest things are encountered or overheard. Amy's voice – he was fairly certain it was Amy's voice – echoing around him.

Human beings are always wondering, after we are gone, what will happen to our ideas, our concerns, our passions? Who will care, and carry on our cause? Many things die with the individual. But some things seem to reach out of time and demand that we pick them up again, demand that their unfinished business be addressed. They shoot the clocks out of our towers, as though furious with time itself.[35]

Whoever spoke these words – if anyone actually did at all – they gave voice to a sadness and a loss that was no personal matter, but rather, a sadness at what we all had lost as human beings, what history took from us, or prevented us from achieving – the missed

---

35 The reference here is, I believe, to an incident from the July Revolution of 1830, when, at the outbreak of the insurrection, Paris's clock towers were fired upon, simultaneously, from a variety of directions.

opportunities, the stolen chances – the poverty of what we have collectively been left with, a miserly bequest at best.

16

Dio placed his bike in one of the *Bicing* racks, locking it into place, and wandered out onto the beach. He stood in the sand for some time and looked at the sea. The sand was thick and red under his feet. The sea before him sparkled in the sun and he thought how this was the Mediterranean sea, a very famous and historical body of water, in which many of history's most famous personages had swam or across which they had sailed to fight wars or take lovers. He tried to think of those famous people, but struggled to come up with many names. Caesar? Christopher Columbus?[36]

He looked around the beach and saw a few people lying in the sun, but not many. It wasn't hot, exactly, but a nice spring day and these must be early-season bathers, perhaps tourists, Dio mused, from England or northern countries who *did* think it was hot today. He looked at the tracks some vehicle had left in the sand, and back at the boardwalk where there were cafés and, further up the beach, some tall apartment towers and gleaming modern buildings. Behind him there were some benches, on the edge of the beach, which he presently repaired to, thinking he would wait for Amy. She was sure to find him here eventually, though he still had the strange feeling of not quite wanting to be found – the pleasure of hiding in plain sight.

Dio took off his shoes and dug his feet into the sand. He had been told by someone, he couldn't remember who, that it smelled at

---

36 For myself, I think of Cervantes and the battle of Lepanto, his capture by Algerian corsairs.

the city beaches, but he didn't find this to be true. It was much, much worse in the Barri Gotic, where one walked in and out of the powerful stench of sewage. But here at the beach, the air was fresh, with a steady breeze coming in off the sea.

Some larger waves presently rumbled against the beach (a boat of some kind must have passed, but Dio hadn't noticed), and he thought how the sound of the waves was like words – words of the sea, he said to himself, words of the origins of ourselves, and he thought of Ramon's poem, pale, lost, and forgotten Ramon, whose words still somehow reached across the years like glassy light that divided the sea as it lay there between now and then. Suddenly Dio recalled another line from the poem – *with wind we communicate subterfuge* – was that right, he wondered? What does it mean – to *communicate subterfuge*? Dio wasn't sure, but he stared at the beach, and watched a woman in a yellow shawl pass, singing softly to herself, as though she were creating her own world with each step she took across the sand, and Dio thought and imagined this and other things too as he sat and watched the sea and people come and go on the beach.

He remembered something else someone had said – someone these past few days he was sure, but did not recall who exactly. (Words kept coming back to him like this – as though he'd been so overwhelmed with information that there was a delay in processing all that he had heard.) That Ramon had wanted *to blast open the continuum of history*. Was that right? He thought of the woman in the hat – had she said this to Amy at the reception? Or had Amy related her saying this, in the car? Or was it from Luis's daughter – Coleen – from her email? He did not appreciate the unreliability of his memory. It seemed, in these few overwhelming days, that he had lost the ability to pin things down, to attach words to the people who spoke them.

Dio had waited for at least an hour when he began to realize Amy would probably not find him. He put his shoes back on, stood, and walked onto the boardwalk. He looked up and down the strip, feeling the sand in his shoes, which he could have done a better job of shaking out. There were people walking, people on bicycles, a woman with a stroller, two rollerbladers. Dio scrutinized the bicyclists absently.

As he stood there, looking up and down, he noticed a man sitting on a nearby bench, regarding him. He had black, spiky hair standing tall and thick on his head. His nose and mouth were covered by a white medical mask, or a dust mask like a carpenter would wear. Perhaps he didn't want to breathe something in the air. Or was worried about contagion, or pollution. His white shirt was mostly open and moved in the breeze, and he wore black rumpled pants, and sandals. He nodded at Dio, who nodded back, then looked away, embarrassed for having stared. He decided to walk in the opposite direction, and as he did so, he glanced once more over his shoulder. The man with the mask was walking towards him. Dio stopped and waited. The other man approached and said hello. Dio greeted him, and the man asked where he was from. Dio told him, and the stranger said he was from Peru, and that he'd thought Dio was South American. The man held out his hand and introduced himself as Poco Yamamoto.

Dio thought about this name as Poco told him that he'd been studying at the university for a few semesters, but that he missed Lima and was going to return soon. Maybe it was the gleaming towers of San Isidro, where his father worked, or the view from the Cerro San Cristobal, which he often thought of, and the young people that gathered there at night. He liked the Spanish, he said, but missed things about his home. He was going to be flying back in a few weeks, maybe a month at the latest, and asked when Dio was returning.

Tomorrow morning, Dio said.

Then this is your last night in Barcelona!

Yes, said Dio. He though it was strange talking to a man in a mask. Everything Poco said was just slightly muffled, like a bad connection on the phone.

Then, Poco was saying, you should do something special. Why not come with me and some friends? We're going to go see a film, then to a bar where a band we like is playing later. How about it? Two South Americans in Barcelona. We can show them how it's done!

Dio thought a moment. He wasn't sure *whom* they were going to *show*, or what they'd *show them*. And it was odd, being approached like this, and he wasn't sure about Poco. He remembered Leandro, then looked up the beach and thought he should try to find Amy, go back to his hotel and see if she'd called. Or if she was even waiting there for him. He should say goodbye and thank you to her. Tell her how she had brought a spark and grace to such formal proceedings. Something like that. Words he'd been turning over and over in his mind, which he thought might make an impression on her. But he was tired of everything to do with his anarchist uncle, and the Civil War, and history and mass graves – seeing a movie and going to a bar with some students in Barcelona seemed like a good way to get through this night and get to the plane and home.

Poco filled the silence, pointing back at the beach and announcing that while it looked impressive, it was entirely man-made. You'd think, he said, that this beach had been here for thousands of years like this, pounded by an eternal surf, but this is a new beach. I'm told, he continued, not too many years ago, this was all docks and warehouses and pollution. They cleaned it up – for the Olympics, of course – remade it in a new image, a new commodity. Old world: industry. New world: tourism. Docks to beaches. Presto.[37]

I should go to my hotel, change, Dio began hesitantly.

Yes of course, Poco said, I'll come with you. Where is your hotel?

Dio hesitated again, not sure he was actually agreeing to go with his new acquaintance, but then gave in with a shrug.[38]

On the square by the big cathedral.

The Placa de Seu. Good. We can follow the Via Laietana.

Poco pointed along the beach and they began to walk. Dio felt strange. This had happened so quickly and unexpectedly, and he felt powerless to resist. Unable to make a choice of his own. Like someone else was in control – not necessarily Poco – but someone other than Dio was making decisions for him and directing his body to move and his mouth to form compliant words.

Poco spoke almost without stopping. He told Dio that his parents, Sansei Japanese-Peruvians, had given him two choices for a year studying abroad: Japan, where his ancestors came from, or Spain, his country's cultural home. He could tell his father, Arturo, who spoke almost no Japanese, wanted him to go to Japan. This would have made his grandmother, who was raised by very

---

37 There is, perhaps, a complex theory of the "event" embedded here, but it would be too much of a digression to go into it at this point.

38 They say the fall of the Berlin Wall began when a border guard let people pass from the east to the west, opening the gate with a shrug.

Japanese, first-generation immigrants, happy. But Poco wanted to write, like his father did, and deepen his understanding of Spanish literature and culture. So he chose Spain. He thought this secretly made his father happy, despite what he chose to reveal on the surface. But he wasn't sure. There had been a new era of pride in being Japanese-Peruvian, since Fujimori's presidency.[39] His father wanted his son to have a prominent career in Peruvian public life. The ties to Japan were important, but mostly only within the family. The ties to Spanish culture, and the ability to demonstrate a cultured knowledge of Spanish art and history – this would serve his son best in public life.

And do you know what I have been studying here, Poco asked?

No, Dio hesitated, suspecting there was a trick.

Catalan language and culture! Catalan! My parents have no clue, they think I'm in Spain so it must be Spanish I'm studying. But it's not Spanish at all! I have Catalan friends and we eat Catalan food. We follow the work of Catalan filmmakers. Maybe it was Gaudi, those buildings like they climbed up out of the earth and sea, or fell in a cloud of birds from the sky, or like the earth dressed itself up in bones and bird's wings to parade through the streets.

Dio wanted to ask why Poco wore the mask, but couldn't bring himself to, or find the opportune moment. Truthfully, it was almost impossible to get a word in. They had left the beach and were walking up the Via Laietana, the smell of sewage occasional-

---

39 This seems unlikely: Fujimori left office in disgrace, and has subsequently been charged and convicted of a number of abuses of power while president. Still, I can only begin to guess what it must be like to have your community's hopes raised so high, and then dashed again so swiftly.

ly wafting past. Was this the reason for the mask? Was Poco's nose too sensitive, or maybe he had respiratory problems? It didn't seem to matter. Poco kept on talking, his voice lightly muffled, gesturing and sometimes laughing as he led Dio up through the Barri Gotic.

My ancestors had been fishermen and farmers. Then we became professionals. But in between, during the Second World War, my grandparents had been interned in American concentration camps. Strange that Peru, the country that had already become home for my grandparents (one was born there, the other came as a baby) would hand us all over to the Americans! Dumping them in with Japanese-Americans who had similarly been dispossessed, in Texas for two years. My grandparents could speak broken Japanese to the American Japanese – but not English, and the Japanese Americans couldn't speak Spanish. Some Peruvian Japanese must have spoken mostly Spanish – Spanish and a little Japanese at least – and they were there with other Japanese who possibly no longer had a shared language. Now I'm here learning Catalan! I find this all very funny. Very strange. We are simultaneously more and less connected to each other every day. We recognize each other as scattered remnants. But really, what links us, one to another?

Half of the time Dio could barely catch what Poco was saying, with the crowds on the sidewalks bustling along beside them and the traffic on the Via Laietana, all horns and shouting. So there were other things Poco said, about students he had befriended and films or a filmmaker he knew, and movies he'd seen in Lima and some comparison he made to the films he'd been watching here in Barcelona, all of which Dio only half got the sense of. Did he say his girlfriend was studying film? Or did he mention a girlfriend at all? Did he say something about samurai films in Spanish? What is a *spaghetti western* (the English words coming out of

nowhere)? Dio just nodded and followed along, occasionally trying to interject something, though Poco simply cut him off saying
Yes, yes, like I was saying, this or that movie, and on and on he
went.

At one point Poco stopped mid-sentence to point at the buildings
they were passing. Look at these stores, he said. This whole area is
being gentrified.

They had turned onto a narrow street where old buildings had
glossy and bright new ground-level stores, the floor-to-ceiling
windows displaying stylish products, all shining leather and
ragged jeans.

I'm told this used to be total crap along here – drugs, addicts and
abandoned buildings. Now (Poco pointed as they walked) – Zara,
Mexx, Diesel, Prada (he shook his head) – incredible. Only the
rich live up there now, Poco said, fixing Dio with an odd and pen-
etrating look and pointing up at the buildings above the stores,
where presumably fashionable and newly refurbished condos
were located. Only those, he went on, who can afford what this
whole city is becoming. Money – you know – that one thing we
all share, to varying degrees, of course. Dio nodded, not sure what
he was supposed to make of this new lesson, but they hurried on.
Would he have to pay for this tour? Maybe that was what all this
was about. He'd heard of hustlers working tourists over like this
before.

When they arrived at the square, people were moving in every
direction and pigeons scurried beneath their feet. They crossed in
the sun, a piece of paper blowing past them, and stopped in front
of the hotel. Poco told Dio to go inside – he would wait out here –
and without waiting he sat down at the café and kept talking, as if

to no one. Dio hesitated a moment, looking across at the cathedral shrouded in scaffolding, then turned and went inside.

17

He asked at the desk if he had any messages. The clerk – the old man who had checked him in three days before – gave him a long, disapproving look, then said, without checking, no he did not. Dio shrugged, glanced around the lobby, and went up to his room.

Inside he bolted the door and threw himself on the bed. He wondered if he could see the café below from his window, but knew that it wasn't possible. Should he go back outside? Maybe if he stayed here Poco would just leave, or maybe he'd find someone else to talk at and drag along on whatever exploits he had planned. Dio looked at the blank television but didn't feel like turning it on. So he looked back up at the crack in the ceiling. It really was a huge crack. Why didn't he see light through it, or hear the people above moving around, talking or fucking? It almost looked as though something small could fall right through it and land on Dio's lap. Some coins or an olive or a message on a small, crumbled piece of paper.

He got up, went to the bathroom, washed his face, and then changed his clothes. His last clean shirt and underwear, which he had intended to save for the plane.

He looked out the window at the square, half imagining he'd see Poco wandering away. People and pigeons. The sun high, late afternoon now. He should have arranged to fly home today – the extra time was unnecessary. But he hadn't been sure what he would need to do while in the city dealing with his uncle (it turned out, next to nothing, in any formal, legal sense). Now it was like a little holiday he was having, a small caesura in his normal life, like when he went to the conference in California, and visited his sister, and sat in a hotel bar drinking an American beer and maybe smoking a cigar and watching the blond waitress move swiftly amongst the tables, her breasts almost spilling out of her top. A few strangely quiet days without his family. A few days living some other life that was, and at the same time wasn't, his. A televised version. With actors. Blasted out of context.

He wondered if there was any way of contacting Amy. He should try. Hadn't she left a number? Or ... the ministry? He looked in his wallet, in the pockets of his jacket. No, he couldn't remember having a number. If she wanted to say goodbye to him, she would call the hotel. She would leave a message for him. She was his host and it was her responsibility. He felt like he knew nothing about her really – and she knew everything about him. Or so it seemed. She had made all this so ... personal and intimate. Death, and grieving what he didn't know he had in the first place. Poetry and architecture. He looked outside again, and then, resigned, again feeling like someone else had control of his will, like someone else was making all the decisions, some strange inner-voice he couldn't hear but could feel, like the little claws of a hamster pushing against a wheel inside, he picked up his jacket, made sure his key was in his pocket, and left his room.

18

Poco was waiting where Dio had left him, either still talking, or simply picking up the thread wherever he had left it the moment he saw Dio approach tentatively. Poco stood and motioned Dio to follow him. They left the square and headed west through the narrow entrance into the Portal de L'Angel, in the direction Dio had thought he heard a choir singing the first day he sat in the square.

Poco was telling Dio about the film they were going to see, where Poco's friends were waiting for them. At least, he was fairly certain it was the film they were going to see. Obviously the Peruvian had seen it many times, possibly even studied it at the university. While Poco spoke Dio was wondering whether you really could describe a movie to someone – wasn't this always a disappointing and fruitless exercise? One had to see films, not hear about them or read about them.

It's a strange film, strange for Eliastrel[40] at least, because it has such *normative* elements – historical context, a character we follow for much of the story, even a story itself – all elements usually more or less absent from Eliastrel's films. There are the director's signatures, certainly – the fact that the crucial moment occurs off-screen, a wounded and moaning dog writhing just on the edge of a camera shot, the almost complete absence of women (though women's voices are, as usual, overheard – or used as voice-over – we won't go *near* the feminist critique here) – but the rest is strangely … normal. Although the film ranges all over a variety of times and places – peasant uprisings in Germany and England, barricades thrown up in Paris streets, Mayan activists in balaclavas blockading a road to a gold mine in Guatemala – the key concluding scene is set during the Civil War (no Spanish filmmaker, avant-garde or not, would have chosen such a setting even ten years ago). The main action, which involves the taking of a small Aragonese village, is shot using almost exclusively non-professional actors – people who actually live in the village where the shooting took place (another Eliastrel signature).

---

40   See the filmography in the section of "documents." I have seen only one Eliastrel film myself, and it troubled and frustrated me deeply. But that seemed to be the intention.

Dio wasn't sure about the name. Elias Trell? Eli Estrelle? Either way, he had never heard of him.

They were walking along one side of the Placa de Catalunya now, on the Passeig de Gracia, and Dio lost track of Poco's muffled voice for a few minutes, remembering instead Amy's rendition of Ramon's life, and the Telefonica wrapped in its white plastic, as though preserved against time, kept from spoiling under the Spanish sun. This was the square Ramon and the boot factory workers stormed; this was where they battled the Spanish army. There was a time when shots rang out here and mortar explosions and bodies lay all over the square where tourists now strolled and pigeons wandered and flowers grew in large beds and Dio and his young Peruvian friend were dragged along by unseen historical forces. Dio looked around, wondering which street the anarchists had come in from, where the soldiers had fled, what jubilation must have followed. Did the ghosts of past struggles still linger? Could he hear them now? Was there some echo of Ramon's poem still vibrating in an iron railing, the fibre of a tree? All was horns and traffic sounds, voices, amongst which he picked up on Poco's again, the Peruvian, having stopped to cross the Ronda de Sant Pere, turning to Dio to emphasize a point with a distinct hand gesture.

Like this, he said, raising his arm, he comes, completely naked through the smoke and fragments flying up from explosions, walking right through the middle of chaos with a red flag in his hand.

Dio stared at him. What was he talking about?

The light changed and they crossed, Poco continuing to talk.

Filmed like the Odessa Steps scene from *The Battleship Potemkin*. An homage – though there have been plenty of those – this time, the baby carriage being replaced by a dolly with a camera on it, coming down the steps ahead of the figure with the flag. A little heavy-handed, admittedly, a little too postmodern, in its arch self-referentiality, for this post-postmodern moment, but you have to see it before you can say that, you know? Actually *see* it, with your own eyes.

But this is the amazing thing, Poco continued. Some of the peasants living in the village take roles as peasants – playing themselves, more or less, only seventy years ago, during the war. Other peasants take roles as Franco's soldiers. There's this scene where the peasants, once the anarchists have liberated the village, sit down and discuss the values of collectivization. Really, the pros and cons of private versus collective ownership of the land. You see the men, but only hear the women – classic Eliastrel. Only, it's amazing, these amateur actors, with no scripted lines, and they can debate ideological fine points like professors at the university. But that's still not what's truly incredible.[41]

They had stopped now in front of a small theatre. Poco looked about briefly and then continued.

The truly incredible thing is the peasants who took the roles of fascists. Apparently, at the end of the day's shooting, the peasants playing peasants would go back to their homes and do chores, feed their kids, their goats, whatever. Their normal routines. Ready to get up and work again in the morning. To go on being what they really were – peasants. But the peasants playing fas-

---

41 The scene described here sounds suspiciously like one in Ken Loach's *Land and Freedom*.

cists would ignore their usual chores and habits. They would keep their uniforms on. They would go to the tavern and drink. They would go out and harass the other peasants. Go to their homes and search and interrogate them. Maybe rough some of them up. Police them. There were, in the weeks of filming, apparently several rapes and numerous beatings. The soldiers never took their uniforms off, day or night, shooting or not shooting. Method acting. Can you believe it?

Dio nodded. It was strange.

Presently, a young man and woman approached them and greeted Poco. Poco introduced Dio as his *friend*. The woman's name was Delfina, and she had blond hair (dyed, Dio thought) and a small scar by the corner of her mouth. The man was named Fausto. He was short, thick and gruff, his hairline only just above his eyebrows, where a deep crease furrowed his abbreviated forehead. His eyes were small and deep-set. They nodded at Dio, barely taking him in, and told Poco that the film had started over an hour ago. Poco didn't seem surprised or disappointed. He gestured everyone to follow and continued talking as they set off along a side street.

So what does this tell us, Dio? About human nature, huh? Tell everyone to be socialists and they become socialists. Tell them to be fascists, and they're fascists. That simple?

Dio shrugged, but he didn't think Poco noticed.

I want to make experiments, Dio. Social experiments. There have been great eras, in history, of human social experiments. But not for a long time now. Now, we must try something again. However strange it may seem. We must see again what ways we can be together. What exchanges we can make. What transactions. The time is ripe for this – the time of crisis is a time for experiments. This is the magic of Eliastrel. He makes experiments – actual experiments, with real people (not actors) as the subjects of his experiments – and films the outcomes. The process. The unexpected – what could never have been predicted. Because everything is so damn predictable, and all the old methods tired and worn out.

Several times Dio looked over his shoulder at Delfina and Fausto. They followed Poco silently, seeming to listen, but as though listening to something they had heard very many times before, or knew in some way by heart. They trudged, really, like soldiers on a forced march, glumly staring at the ground.

Dio could not help thinking there was some invisible force at work. Something that – virtually unrecognized – had grown out of all proportion. Or – because it had grown so vast – one could no longer discern its boundaries, its limits. So – not quite invisible – it was simply pervasive, ubiquitous, blatant and covert at one and the same time. Its machinery was everywhere – all teeth and hair.

Do you know where I was born, Dio? Poco asked.

In … Lima, I assume….

No. In prison.

Poco here fixed Dio with a particular look. Again Dio wondered about Poco's mask.

In prison?

Yes, in the women's prison in Chorrillos. My mother was a member of the Shining Path.[42] You know the Shining Path? You've heard of them? Good. She was Shining Path. Or at least, she was helping them. Letting them use her apartment in the Miraflores district. Hide weapons there. Have clandestine meetings. That sort of thing. She wanted to help make things better in Peru – she was young and idealistic, like us. (*Us*, Dio wondered? He must mean his fellow students.) Perhaps one of the militants was her lover. It doesn't matter. She was arrested and sentenced to twenty years, as a terrorist. Twenty years. My father was her lawyer, and they met while he was working on her appeal, after she had been incarcerated already for a number of years. And he got her out, after serving a little less than ten years. But I was conceived on a *conjugal visit*, you know? And I lived my first three years in jail with my mother and all the other prison women. They were raising me collectively, all those women, all of them so excited to have a *bambino* to care and live for. I must have been terribly popular. There. That's my secret. For my parents, it is *the* big, dark secret. One that can damage your future *opportunities*, as my father would say, plotting things from his desk in San Isidro.

They had slowed now, and Poco turned to look at the buildings they were passing, seemingly satisfied to have revealed his secret. Dio didn't know what to think about any of this, or why Poco felt compelled to reveal this last detail. Or how it fit with anything else he had been told.

Look at this building, Poco suddenly exclaimed, coming to a stop in the street for a moment and then without further hesitation plunging in at what appeared to be a restaurant's door. Dio slowed,

---

42 "Sendero Luminoso," a Marxist insurgent guerrilla organization long struggling against the Peruvian government.

trying to look up at the building as he had been instructed, but he was carried forward by Delfina and Fausto before he could see much. Inside, Poco had already taken the first table. The place was empty. Cheap chairs and battered tables. Strange ornaments and pictures which Dio could not quite make out hung on the walls. Figures of animals? People in festival costumes? Dio and the others filed in silently and sat down. A waitress came with four beers (though no order had been placed) and put them on the table without a word, returning to the back of the room, the kitchen or somewhere out of sight. Delfina and Fausto drank, as did Dio – slowly and mechanically, and a little stunned – but Poco just watched. Dio thought he was smiling behind his mask, but couldn't be sure. He kept looking at Poco's cold beer, and wondering when the Peruvian was going to take a drink, and what he would look like with his mask off – if he took his mask off. There might have been music coming from somewhere. Was this the bar – the party Poco had mentioned? It certainly didn't look like much of a place. And he couldn't imagine live music being performed in here.

Dio is from La Ciudad, Poco said softly, nodding. Delfina and Fausto looked at Dio carefully, as though trying to verify or evaluate this piece of information. He is an urban planner, and has been to the architecture school[43], Poco continued. Dio didn't recall telling him this – in fact, he remembered having few opportunities to say anything at all – but he nodded just the same, as though he needed whatever credibility he could muster, however fraudulent and unexpected. Delfina and Fausto exchanged an inscrutable

---

43 La Ciudad's Escuela de Arquitectura de los Andes is known for its politicized students and faculty and the radical experiments in design produced by these same practitioners. Gloria Personne, an avid amateur student of architecture, had long held a keen interest in the school, and had corresponded with some of its scholars.

glance. Fausto took a cell phone from his pocket and began to study it absently, scrolling through something with his thumb. Was he going to Google Dio's name?

Poco then spoke as though his earlier conversation had merely been held in abeyance for a moment, interrupted by the long parenthesis of these other niceties. He also spoke with a kind of excitement, as though they had actually *just seen* the film he was now carefully deconstructing.

So some peasants become fascists because they have been told to do so. Others are anarchists, because this is what they were told – by someone they assumed, or took, to have the authority to so instruct them – someone they have given the power to make their reality for them. Now, I ask you, are we all so pliable? Are we all such simple clay, blank slates awaiting an author/director to tell us what we must do?

Poco paused and looked at Dio expectantly. Delfina and Fausto were looking too, Delfina's beer glass held in the air just below her mouth, and Fausto's thumb hovering over the keypad of his cell phone.

Well, Dio began awkwardly, I guess there's such a thing as ... as human nature, isn't there? Some basic ... things everyone more or less ... believes in? Or feels compelled by? Things which we are born with, and which don't really change?

Like what, Poco asked, sounding disinterested. Delfina and Fausto seemed disappointed too, and returned to their distractions.

Dio thought for a moment. I don't know. Procreating? Protecting, caring for children? One's family? You know, instincts. Survival.

Basic needs and urges.

Bourgeois bullshit, Poco snapped. What about homosexuals? Do you think they feel this urge to procreate?

Dio was taken aback. I ... I don't know. Sometimes ... they adopt....

Poco sighed. He still hadn't taken a sip of his beer, while the others were half-finished. Poco's manner had changed since they had met up with his two followers. He had become edgier, less at ease and friendly. More aggressive.

Fausto turned his phone over and over in his hands, or held it in one hand and absently rubbed it against his chin and neck, like an electric razor.

Why do things not change, Dio – why is there always the same pattern emerging: privilege and inequality? Winners and losers? Oppressors and the oppressed?

Dio shook his head slowly, staring at the last remnants of foam on his dwindling beer.

We must discuss the will, Poco went on.

The will?

Yes, the will. How, for instance, do you turn your body? Have you pondered this? You are walking along, and you turn to the left as you walk, to avoid a dog or someone walking towards you or some shit on the ground. How do you do that? It's not like a bike. On a bike, you turn the handlebars, which turn the front wheel.

The shape of the tire on the road, and the friction, causes the bike to turn. And the rest of the bike, with you on it, follows. But that's not how your body turns when walking. It's not the feet that turn first, and the rest of the body follows. Pay attention next time you are walking. Is it your hips? Your shoulders, head? No. Turn any of these, and you can still make yourself shuffle forwards, walking like some sort of misfit. In turning the body, there are dozens, hundreds of small subtle things that happen in an instant that allow you to turn. All the parts working together by some hidden mechanism of communication, of information moved from cell-to-cell. Now think about a whole culture, a whole society. How does it turn in a particular direction? How many parts need to be engaged to turn this monster? How many millions, maybe billions of subtle things must coordinate to turn something that large and complex? And with a culture, no one mind says – watch out for the shit on the ground! Turn left!

Poco paused, nodding. Dio shifted uncomfortably in his seat, glancing around the café quickly. A painting on the wall to his left displayed a close-up of someone shouting, a hand cupped beside their mouth for amplification. The person wore a red banana, across which was written, not in its usual font, the word *coke*.

They have done studies, the neuroscientists, you know, Poco continued, leaning forward and looking directly into Dio's eyes. Scans of the brain, with sensors that measure neurological activity while certain mental tasks are being performed. They find that altruism, for example, you know what altruism is? Well, altruism is located in the frontal lobe (that's the part of the brain that's active when you ponder doing something altruistic, or feel empathy, things like that) – one of the newest or youngest parts of the brain, in evolutionary terms. The most recently evolved, if you will. While basic responses like fear, anger, lust, are deeper in the mammalian and reptilian brain that lies beneath. Fight-or-flight stuff. So it may be that we have evolved from a more reactive creature to one shaped by social relations themselves, one whose brain has grown to allow it to think of, and have empathy for, others. To consider community as part of its necessary means of survival. So we are adapting to the fact of, and to better enable, our social lives. Becoming aware of what it means to be in a community, even to be a particular species. And the brain is growing to accommodate these new social functions, this awareness of and care for the group, to be able to empathize with an other, someone or something that is not us but is maybe *like* us, and similarly feels what we feel. Human history, you know, is very young, very new. If the history of all life on earth formed a single, twenty-four-hour day, human beings would have arrived only in the last few seconds of that day. That's what they say. We are small, insignificant. Latecomers to the goings-on of this planet. Like party crashers who have arrived with a great drunken cry, knocking over the table that was set for a banquet for all.

Poco raised a hand and adjusted his mask slightly.

Do you read novels, Dio?

Novels?

Yes, novels, stories, works of fiction.

Sometimes....

History is over. I think everything, everything human, relies upon fiction at some basic level now. Maybe that's the simple clay we are made of. The clay of stories. Marketing a product is a story. Raising a family is a story. Living in a nation is a story, you see?

Being of a particular race or ethnicity. Sexuality. Politics and economics – those are big stories we keep telling ourselves, hoping something will come out right – happy endings and all that.

What is your story Dio? Hmm? I think I've heard it before. I'm pretty sure I know it already. You tried to be a good guy and do what's right, but really you were just stuck in the mechanism all along, and somewhere deep down you knew it. What we need is something utterly new, something we haven't thought of already, you know? People with the power to change things. People brave enough to believe they really have the power, and permission, to change things, to break with what has gone before and produce a new arrangement of the things that make up this world, to turn suddenly and start a different story. That's what's so important in Eliastrel. He's not afraid to change direction partway there, to suddenly look somewhere else for the thing he hasn't found yet, like moving to another room, another city. He shows us the strange relationships between disparate things. These days, I'm between stories, watching for that turn, while trying to live the best way I can while the old story other people are still trying to live in crumbles around us. Meanwhile, Dio, your time is done.

My time?

Yes. All of you. You relentless liberals, so convinced you might lose something you never had. Your world is split open. Cleaved. Now there are only militants and millionaires.

Poco rose from his chair.

Do you believe in happy endings, Dio? I would like to – we all would like to. But they are rare. And do you know what? I think the happiness part is irrelevant. It's endings that are the real problem. Because nothing ends. Everything's just some wreckage in a dump somewhere, still lingering in some spent form. Think about that, Dio. Think about where and how you might linger.

Poco now took his mask down, slowly and deliberately, even dramatically, with both hands. Dio didn't know what he expected, but Poco's face looked average enough. Although not very Japanese, he thought, whatever that might mean. Poco lifted his glass of beer and drained it in one go. Then, smiling, wiping his mouth with the back of his hand, he replaced the empty glass on the table, turned and casually walked towards the back of the restaurant and disappeared.

Now Fausto got up too and, after fixing Dio with what he took to be a threatening glare, and rubbing his cell phone against his chin again, followed Poco, muttering something about how Delfina would take care of him.

When they were both gone Delfina leaned forward, a strange and excited look on her face.

You should go now, she whispered. Or get in all the way. It's up to you – but you should decide. And probably you should go, if you are going to go – now's your chance. These parties … (here she made a vague wave of her hand) – there are always some strangers like yourself. Someone from out of town. Preferably an American. Or an Englishman. Someone foreign. And they have this choice to make.

Dio stared at Delfina, then back into the restaurant, where Poco and Fausto had disappeared, then back at Delfina. He was finding it hard to take in what he was being told.

What – what choice, he asked?

Delfina smiled, the scar at the side of her mouth rippling. The choice to go or to stay, stupid.

She paused. Or, if you prefer, the choice … to be a peasant, or a fascist!

At this Delfina grinned, sitting back, quite satisfied with the analogy she had produced.

Dio looked at the empty glasses on the table, trying to think. The mood around him, the whole atmosphere of this day and even his three days in Barcelona, had suddenly changed. Menace had appeared out of nowhere. Meaningless and wholly unpredictable menace. They sat in silence for a moment. To delay, or perhaps to turn the conversation back to an earlier, less strained moment in its evolution, Dio asked what the name of the film was – the film they had missed.

There are two versions, Delfina answered at once. The first was called *The Second Undertaker*.[44] It refers to the structure of the film, how it turns back on itself, or turns itself inside out. Breaking off and starting over again. Or like one film growing, unexpectedly, within the body of another – a rogue sub-narrative destroying its host from within. Halfway through – right after the scene where the peasants discuss whether or not to collectivize – there is a rough cut to the present day. A man comes out of a theatre, and complains that the film he has been watching has ended halfway through. An acquaintance appears at his side and takes him

---

44 The reference to *Don Quixote* here should be fairly obvious. It's surprising "the director," mentioned here, isn't named Cide Hamete Benegeli!

to another theatre, where a documentary about the making of the first film is showing. In this film a man, referred to simply as *the director*, is being interviewed by none other than Eliastrel himself (who has never, in nineteen films, once appeared in his own features, or even done an interview or made an appearance at Cannes[45]). The only reason we know it is Eliastrel is that his name appears as a caption on screen. The *director* claims to have made the film *The Second Undertaker*, about the liberation of a village during the Civil War. He is an Arab, and claims it is an allegory about Israeli-Palestinian relations. He tells Eliastrel what happens, and that's pretty much the end.

Dio had not expected this return to Poco's lecture, but it didn't surprise him somehow that Delfina could step into her master's shoes.

That version has been circulating in a pirated copy, though most of us believe Eliastrel was behind its covert release. Apparently dissatisfied with the film, or maybe his backers were dissatisfied, Eliastrel completely re-cut it, and added a lot of new scenes. He completely got rid of the whole second theatre/documentary interview stuff. The new version, which is a far superior film, is entitled *The Red Album*. It follows a bumbling documentary film-maker, named Ramon, who travels through time to many revolutionary times and places – with Che and Fidel in the jungles of Cuba; building a barricade out of paving stones in the Rue St. Maur in Paris in 1848; occupying St Georges Hill with the Diggers in 1649; and so on and so forth. He interviews people, hears their stories, takes down details, and offers his summaries directly into the camera. He has a pet bear which chases cops down a street in

---

45 The filmography, below, suggests otherwise. It's also highly likely the "Eliastrel" identified in this version of the film is an actor.

St. Petersburg, allowing Ramon and Lenin to escape into a cellar. The climax is when Ramon covers the battle during the Civil War. Everywhere he goes he gets involved in the action and interviews the key players. At one point – really, it's my favorite scene – Ramon gets into an argument with Subcommandante Insurgente Marcos, the Zapatista, about the revolutionary potentiality of the Internet. Marcos wants to talk about poetry, but Ramon insists our struggles will now take place in the virtual realm.

Dio stared at the empty beers on the table. Ramon?

Ramon. A Spanish anarchist and poet, who goes in search of the roots of social change. He has a pet bear named Luis. They are a little like Tintin and Snowy, you know? Only radicals.

Delfina leaned close again. Dio watched the scar at the corner of her mouth ripple. Look, she continued, we should get down to business. You either buy in to the experiment, or you don't. It's up to you. If you stay, you get to see the places upstairs. This neighbourhood, she said, gesturing around them, so close to the theatre where all the independent and art-house films show, has barely begun being gentrified. Soon, all the best stores will be moving in. The Gap, Tommy Hilfiger, Starbucks. Tourists will come into these streets with their money. Gay people. Creative people. People like Poco – trendsetters. Maybe a film festival will be held. Celebrities, walking their infinitely small dogs. And the apartments in this building will be in high demand. It is a rare opportunity you have here, Dio – not everyone gets brought in like this, for an exclusive viewing. I think you should stay – I think you have already decided to stay – and I will show you the place, and Fausto will arrange the financing, and you'll have yourself a perfect little vacation spot for whenever you come to Europe, or send your business associates. Maybe you'll even decide to move in yourself, and stay permanently, hm? That's what I think – no one in his right mind would leave now. No one.

At this, Delfina brought a brochure up from somewhere under the table and placed it in front of Dio. The glossy cover showed a fashionable couple relaxing at the iron railing of a balcony, looking down into a narrow street, wine glasses in their hands. The writing at the top was in English, but below the image, in smaller print, it read in Spanish, *A Revolution in European Living*.

Dio still couldn't quite fathom what was happening. He tried to concentrate on the empty glasses in front of him, beside the brochure, as though the explanation might lie there amongst them and in the wet rings on the glossy table. Delfina, for her part, sat back smiling and took a cigarette out of her purse. Dio looked around once more, then said, almost in a whisper to himself, I thought he was a student.

Delfina took a long drag on her cigarette, fixing Dio with a piercing look. He is a student, she said, but he still has to pay his bills. Poco, he likes being avant-garde *and* making money.

Somehow, Dio found the strength, or more accurately, the agency, to move. He stood up without a word, and without glancing at Delfina, and walked out of the restaurant.

19

The sun was low in the sky now, casting long shadows in the street, the sky a strange blue uncommonly seen over the Mediterranean. A South American sky, big and sharp. Dio looked over his shoulder several times (he couldn't help it) as he walked back towards the Placa de Catalunya. In the Barri Gotic, he found the quietest and narrowest streets. Almost empty. Long shadows draped about and light spilled from shops, voices echoed from balconies above. He wasn't sure he was going to be able to find his hotel, but eventually he did, wandering into the square in front of the cathedral from an angle he had never approached before. A sign by a rough wall, which Dio stopped to read, said that it dated from Roman times. The name Barcelona comes from *barca*, meaning boat.[46]

Touching the ancient wall, Dio thought he grasped the specific constellation which his own era formed with that earlier one. Only he wasn't sure what that relation was, or the sense of it fled his mind before he could shape it into words.

Dio went into his hotel and ate. Then he went to sleep. In his dream, Barcelona was a boat, its buildings and parks sprouting from the deck of a vast ship, which leaned sharply to one side, tacking in a strong wind. Angry waters lapped at its sides, and the people in its streets, including Dio, clung to spars and stays that were found at most street corners. A seagull swept between the tipping towers of buildings. Someone fell into the water and disappeared. It might have been Amy. Or Malinche. Dark clouds piled to the stern.

20

In the morning Dio rose early, shaved and showered, and packed his bag. He sniffed clothes before deciding what to pack, what to wear. Yesterday's shirt would have to do. He looked up at the crack in his ceiling before leaving the room.

---

46 This etymology may be spurious, but it seems a bit picky to question the author's imaginative license at this point. We all take our leaps to make ends meet.

At the desk, he checked out (it was the young, polite black woman), then sat by the café entrance in the lobby to wait. He was early, and did not have to meet his cab for another half-hour, maybe 45 minutes. He was always early, always waiting. He half-expected to see someone he knew come into the lobby to say goodbye – Amy or Poco or even Leandro.

He thought about the Peruvian. Everything that came out of his mouth had seemed to be about art and politics and then suddenly – what? He was selling something? Some sort of scam? Dio tried to recall the things Poco had said, looking for clues. Then he wondered what he had told the Peruvian. Was there anything revealing, anything he shouldn't have said? Any indiscretion? Had he told him about Leandro's wife and their little monster? He worried maybe he had, but wasn't sure. For some reason that seemed like an important story, one he needed to keep to himself for a while. One, even, you didn't want to look inside of, no matter how strong the temptation to do so. But that didn't make sense, and he wasn't sure he'd even said more than a few words to Poco the whole time they had been together.

He thought of the strange bar they had entered last night. It was, Dio told himself – trying to sound poetic perhaps – the straight gate through which change might have entered his life. But what kind of change? He wasn't sure. But he felt, now, reconsidering events, that there was something about Poco that was … innocent. That there was something else which was pulling his strings, but which did not taint or pollute his person. Like he was an effect, but not a cause. Part of the surface décor.

Try as he might, Dio could not pin these things down. Really, they were thought processes he had rarely entered into before. He became distracted, and looked around the lobby.

A television was on and several people, including two hotel employees, were watching. Dio didn't pay attention at first, but something made him look back a moment later. The television showed people running through streets, burning, overturned cars, and a helicopter taking off from a deserted square, papers swirling away from its spinning rotor. Then it showed some buildings in a park-like setting, strange, modern buildings, where a vast crowd had gathered, waving banners and signs and flags. Dio thought he recognized the buildings. He stood, leaving his bag behind, and walked towards the television.

A reporter spoke into the camera for a moment (but there was no sound). Then there was an aerial shot of a city with smoke rising from a distant neighbourhood. Tall, concrete apartment buildings loomed over a shantytown spread across a gully beneath them.

It was La Ciudad.

Dio turned to a young man beside him and asked what was happening.

The young man shrugged. A revolution.

There? Dio asked, pointing at the screen. The young man, who worked in the hotel, looked at Dio like he was crazy, or stupid. He looked back at the television, nodding.

A revolution, Dio repeated.

Yes, the employee said. It began the other day, with some architecture students. Then, suddenly, a very organized uprising. The president fled by helicopter (they keep showing that footage – it's good, classic). The parliament's been stormed, thousands of people are in the streets, all that sort of stuff. Now everyone is waiting to see what the army will do.

Dio stared at the television for a moment longer. They were showing the helicopter again. Then a commercial. Mentos.

Dio turned away, walking back towards his bag lying on the lobby floor, past his bag and towards the dark wood of the hotel front desk. He stopped in the middle of the lobby and looked at his feet. He couldn't go home. He knew it, in an instant. The country would be sealed. The airports, borders, everything. He was stuck here, in Barcelona, and for who knows how long. His country had been pulled from under his feet. He should be there. To make sure Ignacio and Malinche were alright, that his girls were alright. He should be home but he wasn't, he couldn't be, he suddenly thought he might never be. He saw then the image of a sword or a flame, a bright slash of light somewhere far off, amidst smoke and police and helicopters, blurring and blinding his inner-vision – a beacon marking a haven or a horror that he had kept inside himself all this time. His feet would not move. Suddenly it was very hard to breathe.

2 · Documentos

Introduction

We have gathered here all the associated documents we could find that might help flesh out Gloria's story, and the story of Ramon Fernandez. Everything, that is, except for my complete translation of the *Quixote Variations*, which must be omitted for copyright reasons (currently being contested by Fernandez's Spanish relatives – although some selections can be found in the first document here – "The Theatre of Criticism"). I can, at least, justify this omission, in part, by reference to my own well-publicized problematization of translation in that omitted document. I will paraphrase some of what I have written there.

Translation is abstraction, and what is "taken out" (to "abstract" is to "remove") is the author of the original. She is abstracted and the translator takes her place and writes as though she *is* the original poet. Or, the translator is the original poet forgetting her original language, and writing as if she had not already written the poem before, in another tongue, in another life. Thus the translator is the poet with amnesia: write; disappear; reappear elsewhere, in a new tongue, a new identity; now write that "same" text again, without any knowledge of having written it already. This is how we must proceed, as though we aren't who we are, as though we are doing something that we are not.

Translation is thus a demand for the impossible. This is where I have arrived after years of struggling with Fernandez's work. It's not exactly a happy place for someone who identifies as a translator to wind up: your professional aspirations are *by definition* impossible. Now what? I will spare the reader the gory details, and get on with the present task.

The reader hoping to find a continuation of Dio's story here in these documents will be sorely disappointed – and we share this disappointment. However, Dio was never Personne's focus; he was incidental, a device, an epiphenomenon, a means for getting at the more crucial story of Fernandez (however lost, obscured and circumscribed that story may ultimately remain). We could speculate that, as an inexperienced novelist, Personne simply got carried away with what ultimately should have been little more than a *preface* to the larger work on Fernandez – a work that she either never wrote, or which is now lost to us. So this is all we have – a meagre bequest.

We hesitate to simply dump all of this upon the reader's lap. Like the contents of a shark's stomach cut open and spilt across a soggy dock, was how Collis put it; I should think more like the contents of an old suitcase, into which books (some with detailed marginalia), newspaper clippings, some rough notes, a sketchbook, and various personal effects of uncertain origin and authenticity had been stowed, long since their putative owner had passed away in some other country where distant lights grew dim. To me, they are glimpses of other, unwritten novels. Collis calls them "a series of digressions and dispersals." I think there isn't anything that's not a digression from something else we could be doing or writing. Something always interrupts and intervenes. Misdirects. For better or for worse, here they are.

"The Theatre of Criticism" is part-essay, part-creative response, part-speculative commentary. It is followed here by the other significant piece of Fernandez scholarship: Stephen Collis's able essay, "The Plebeian Cantos." While I do not agree with all of Collis's conclusions, I recognize the importance of this piece – however controversial – for moving Fernandez studies forward. Next in line is a selection from Personne's "Autobiography" (some parts of which have been previously published). It is an unusual document, and perhaps the best hope we have of understanding the absent author of *The Red Album*.

Poco Yamamoto's "Eliastrel Filmography" more or less fell into our hands: a friend of Collis's found it in some obscure Peruvian film journal, clipped and mailed it to him on the off chance it could be of some use. We were a little uncertain, but the ghost of Fernandez hovers there, and so we have included it here. The translation is mine.

The section of "Documents" concludes with a strange, contemporary story that we include here simply for the sake of doing our due diligence. When seeking permission for the inclusion of Yamamoto's filmography, we were alerted to the existence of what was purported to be a new film treatment penned by none other than Eliastrel himself. A work-in-progress it would seem, how Yamamoto came into possession of it, and what hand he may have had in generating the text (it came to us already translated into English), is a story we will have to save for another time. He, at least, has quite a yarn to spin (the most surprising aspects of which are his claim to have met Eliastrel in Barcelona, from whose own hands he acquired the text – and his offer to hand-deliver the precious manuscript to us in Vancouver, a city which, he noted, he had visited with his father once, "on business," and of which he had "fond memories"). Yamamoto reports that Eliastrel intends to dedicate whatever film he makes from the "script," if he ever does so, to "the timeless memory of Ramon Fernandez." It adds little to our understanding of either Personne or Fernandez, as far as I'm concerned, and seems little more than a sketch. Nevertheless, it does allow us to tie off some loose ends, and as Collis says, the ghost of Fernandez is present in this story too, however fleetingly, floating across the stage of contemporary history, its mounting crises and roiling social movements.

We close, finally, with an appendix of two poems previously published by Collis, which I requested to republish here as a kind of concluding dedication.

While I personally have grave suspicions about narrative as a coercive cultural formation, I am heartened by, and close this short introduction with, these words of Ramon Fernandez: "Even narrative – yes, even the simple telling of events – was once insurgent, once a radical break with the contemplative complacency of a culture of images and idolatry." I hope this is so. It's something to aspire to, if nothing else.

– Alfred Noyes

The Theatre of Criticism:

AN ADAPTATION OF RAMON FERNANDEZ'S QUIXOTE VARIATIONS

Alfred Noyes

Introduction

It is a seemingly off-hand comment – a brief jotting in the Spanish poet Ramon Fernandez's slight and fragmentary archive: "In the theatre of criticism [*el teatro de critica*] we mistake a theatre of war." The comment would seem to be a pronouncement on the state of literary criticism, ironically comparing critical debates to the far more dramatic and disastrous "theatre of war." And it may indeed be so. But another possibility arises when we refer to a little-known notice in *Ambos* (April 1926), the journal edited by Fernandez's friend Manuel Altolaguirre, which announces the printing of a pamphlet by Imprenta Sur entitled "El teatro de critica," authored by none-other than Ramon Fernandez. The notice calls the work a "stunning new manifesto" and includes a brief quotation: "The theatre of criticism is the dromenon of social life; why be surprised if we find in it expressions of affinity alongside critical discriminations?"

My searches to locate this obscure item have been entirely fruitless; after months combing various databases and archives I can only conclude that the pamphlet was never actually printed, or for that matter, even written. It could even be a joke (Altolaguirre was not above such pranks – announcing at one point, in *Poesia* (1932) a "novel by Federico Garcia Lorca," which never appeared and doubtlessly never existed). It is also worth noting that Fernandez, by all accounts, had ceased writing by 1925, after which point his whereabouts are little known (until his reappearance in Barcelona in the mid-1930s).

But there is one other, only recently unearthed piece of evidence: a small packet of letters written by Altolaguirre to his future wife, Concha Mendez, when he was living in Paris (1930-32). One of these letters mentions a visit by a "Ramon," with whom Altolaguirre discusses "the theatre." They visit the critic Pierre Menard, and Altolaguirre records "Ramon" telling Menard that "poets are simply becoming characters in a fiction." What of critics, Menard asks? Ramon responds, "Actors. Actors who want to play the characters poets have become."

If we are to entertain the idea (as I wish to do here) that "the theatre of criticism" was more than an off-hand comment; if, in fact, I am to entertain this phrase conceptually, even theoretically, I am up against a blank wall of historical silence. If Fernandez developed a theory of the theatre (or a theory of criticism – it is a little unclear), why does no one else from that era mention it? Fernandez himself comes up, and his work receives comment in a number of journals. He was friends, in the early 1920s at least, with a wide circle of leading Spanish literati, including Lorca, Altolaguirre and Buñuel. Lorca, especially, had an interest in the theatre; why would Fernandez's interest in, or ideas about, the theatre never have surfaced?

The wise decision here – the circumspect decision – would be to walk away from the theatre of criticism as a topic about which anything else could be said. However, though I am usually just such a circumspect person, I will allow myself to pursue the subject, taking the license which poets have so often relied upon when crossing imaginary frontiers. I quote the physicist Niels Bohr for further permission: "An independent reality in the ordinary physical sense can neither be ascribed to the phenomena observed nor the agencies of observation."

One postulate, then, of the theatre of criticism, is that we too-often delude ourselves with the idea that criticism is real, factual, disinterested, objective, empirical, material, and that the objects studied by criticism are in turn also real, material, empirical, etc. We make up what we say, and we make up the objects we discuss as we say what we are saying about them – despite their fleeting resemblances to things we want to label "real."

The only thing less relevant than poetry today is literary criticism. The theatre of criticism must begin with this postulate above all else. It must embrace its own irrelevance. As it falls *out of the world* we recognize, it must grasp that outside fiercely, and not let go. Its irrelevance *is* its relevance. Its grip is the very nature of terror – that we have left no impression, nor was there anything to impress upon.

The theatre of criticism is entirely fraudulent. It commits crimes against property and veracity. But the gestures it makes, between one fraud and another, are entirely *sincere*. Really. Its claims about the unreal are – strangely *real*.

The theatre of criticism occurs outside institutional spaces and paradigms. If the work you observe displays institutional credentials, or is institutionally sanctioned, it is not the theatre. The theatre is entirely unsanctioned. It occurs in gutters and cafés, badly written blogs and thuggish comments streams. It is "public," thus, it is very nearly invisible, rapidly disappearing, unrecollected. Words spat out of bus stops and drowned in endless traffic.

Sometimes we find ourselves in the theatre of criticism without recognizing it. We call this "networking," or "making contacts." Let's pretend: you review me, I review you. We read each other's poems (barely) and whisper sweet nothings, banal praise. We attend "events" to "see" others and "be seen." This is all the theatre of criticism. Who did you pretend to be today? What writer did you pretend to read? What was your honest pretend reaction?

If poetry has nowhere "real" to be anymore – no space or place of action – and if criticism is doubly "displaced" – then the fictive is the only option left. Let's pretend there's a place for this, OK? You go stage left, I'll go stage right. I wrote a book. You wrote about the book I wrote. Now – action.

In the theatre of criticism, we face the pointlessness of our literary activities and efforts. We exist, there, in pure anxiety, writing with no net (no poet, no critic – no subject, no object – just writing). Doubt is everything in the theatre of criticism. In it, all the negative affects of our literary lives are given free reign. We howl the unalloyed howl of our raw marginality. The theatre of criticism is petty, childish, aggrieved – slighted, jealous, egotistical. It fights over the smallest scraps as though they were all the world's banquet. Turning on itself, its only hope is that "I is another." I is. Theatrically thrown.

The theatre of criticism brays from the margin not because poetry (and criticism) makes nothing happen. In fact, it makes pretend things happen. But it's difficult to separate the pretend from the uselessly "real," and the margin only ever expands. The margin is, in fact, huge now, vast, very nearly the entire world. We're all on the edges. Looking in at what?

The theatre of criticism believes in bogus theories. Because *it is* a bogus theory.

Or – all theories are bogus by definition (and in the theatre revealed as such – in character) – a supposing to know by subjects supposed to know.

Now – let's suppose there's such a theatre.

I have found Ramon Fernandez's *Quixote Variations* to be one of the most fascinating and impossible, fraudulent and complicit poems I have ever read. I have pursued its various editions and versions. I have translated it. I have hoarded and protected it. I have lived with it. I have crushed it under my pillow and woken drooling on its scattered pages. Now, I subject it to its only possible fate – the theatre of criticism. It's yours now too. Open the doors.

*

Characters:

Pierre Menard – a French literary critic
Ramon Fernandez – the dead Spanish poet
Helen Vendler – an American literary critic

Setting:

Possibly an apartment in Paris (or New York), anywhere from 1938 to 2008. There are three objects on the stage: a bookshelf, a wingback chair in front of the bookshelf, and, lying on the floor a few feet in front of the chair, an open, pine coffin. Pierre Menard sits in the chair, hands folded in his lap, legs crossed, studying the audience. It is clear that there is a body in the coffin (that of Ramon Fernandez). Helen Vendler remains offstage throughout.

MENARD: Good evening. My name is Pierre Menard, and I will be speaking tonight about the poetry of Ramon Fernandez – in particular, his acknowledged masterwork, the "Quixote Variations." As a long-time student of Cervantes's great work, I am perhaps better situated to understand Fernandez's undertaking than many others, despite the fact that I am French, not Spanish. It also helps that I met Fernandez, in Paris in 1930, and was able to ascertain certain aspects of his intentions and beliefs that remain beneath the surface of his work, outside of the written word, and thus have been a cause of confusion for many of his readers.

One obvious reading of Fernandez's "Quixote" is to read it as an attack upon, or deconstruction of, Cervantes's masterpiece. Indeed, one could consider it an attack on the very notion of "masterpieces," with the hierarchies they connote and the scarcity they imply. Masterpieces would be impossible in a world without property (they are wholly dependent upon the concept of private property and the scarcity of the particular property of the "masterwork"), so if we are to read Fernandez as a radical poet, even as an anarchist poet (though it is somewhat difficult to clarify the relationship between his literary activities in the early 1920s and his later political activities in the 1930s), we must suppose him to be one opposed to the hierarchical and exclusive notion of the masterpiece. Though he says so nowhere, we must see him as opposed to the very privileged position of the *Quixote* in Spanish literature and culture.

FERNANDEZ (from the coffin):

> Through crushed Saturdays
> And broken Mays

Never with three soft days
Overwhelming us

Having neither marginal
Nor critical remarks

Nothing to register
Delight

That expression
Is eloquence's unreason

Thus I agree to fill
Your margin

And offer a few pages
At the end of your book

Sublime stars and
Aristotle raised

From the dead
For that very purpose

MENARD: The opening lines here can indeed be read as the words of a radical working-class poet bemoaning the lot of an underclass which has all sense of leisure ("Saturdays") and hope ("May," with its invocation of rebirth and revolutionary possibility) "crushed" and "broken." The context, however, immediately shifts, and beginning with the words "Having neither marginal / Nor critical remarks," we are thrown into the Preface of *Don Quixote* and Cervantes's lament for his "bare words." Much of the rest of this poem is comprised of language stripped from Cervantes's great work –

and indeed such literary pilfering and plagiarism might, in fact, be read as a critique of property and the exclusions and privileges assigned to certain texts in the canon.

VENDLER (interrupting from offstage): You are basing your comments on an ideological *a priori* that has nothing whatsoever to do with criticism, the task of which is simply to *describe* the work of art.

MENARD (looking angrily offstage): Vendler – I'm getting there. Please bear with me. (Faces the audience again.) Where was I? Oh yes –

Fernandez's hand has arisen from his coffin, holding an unlit ciga-rette aloft. As Menard continues talking, he gets up, pulls a lighter from his jacket, lights Fernandez's cigarette, and returns to his seat. Fernandez smokes in the coffin.

I am offering the hypothetical and perhaps expected reading: finding evidence of the later political "radical" in the earlier aesthetically "radical" and appropriative work of his bohemian youth. But the tricky part here is that there is no way of knowing exactly what Fernandez's attitude to Cervantes's work – as canoni-cal text or cultural icon – was. Many lesser writers might borrow from a great writer's masterpiece; why should we read Fernandez's borrowings – raw, bald, and blunt as they are – any differently? In fact, in invoking the "friend" from Cervantes's Preface, who offers to assist the author by "agree[ing] to fill / Your margin" and "a few pages / At the end of your book," isn't Fernandez fulfill-ing a supportive and ultimately dedicatory function with regard to the prior work? Isn't he undertaking to in some sense *extend* and *continue* the master's project? Isn't he, in fact, not "critiquing" Cervantes's *Quixote* at all, but rather, acknowledging its priority and declaring a sort of subordination and dependence, or at the very least, an aesthetic affinity?

VENDLER: What do you mean by "aesthetic affinity"?

MENARD (again looking annoyed): That the artistic choices a poet makes can be as much about identifying with a particular source as they can be ... distantiations from or critiques of a predecessor.

VENDLER: You're trying to invoke old, weird Harold Bloom.

MENARD: Not at all. But now that you've called him to mind, certainly. Yes. Most of our models of critique and argument are based upon competition over scarce resources, privacy and individuation, distinguishing the unique, original. These are inflected with capitalist epistemology. But what I'm interested in, and what I think you can see in Fernandez's work, is an expression of authorial or aesthetic affinity. One responds to Cervantes by writing Cervantes – recreating him anew, in a new historical context. And that's what Fernandez was doing. He was *being Cervantes*, if Cervantes were an anarchist poet working in a Barcelona book factory in the twentieth century. What then would he write?

FERNANDEZ (tossing his cigarette butt):

> Beyond
> Water
> Bodies
> Flutter
> Sleeves
> Cry
> Oceans

Masks
Heard
Grinding
Phrases
Songs
Tragic
Spirit
Spain
Sunken
Summer
Vanished
Artificer
Self
Out of
Order

VENDLER: I am curious, Menard, about the fact that Fernandez is such a marginal, minor, even forgettable figure – what is your attraction to his slight body of work? Isn't this just the case of a lesser figure who tried – unsuccessfully – to hitch his wagon to a star?

MENARD (indignant): Are you calling *me* a "lesser figure"?

VENDLER: No, you idiot – Fernandez.

MENARD (self-importantly): We are all "lesser figures" until someone makes masterpieces of our productions.

VENDLER: Good luck then. As for myself, I like to pick the winners.

MENARD: The losers are infinitely more interesting. Anyway, I thought Marjorie Perloff said that?

VENDLER: Misattribution is everything.

MENARD: I must get on with my talk –

FERNANDEZ:

> Born free
> I retired
> So I might continue
> To these solitary hills
> Where only companions
> And sources are ours
> And the clear trees
> Seem of crystal
>
> With wind
> I communicate
> Subterfuge
> And my thoughts
> Go towards absence
>
> I am a distant flame
> And a sword far off
> Having attacked seeing
> They now deceive
> Words demanding
> The impossible
> Speech of windmills

MENARD: Fernandez here appropriates the voice of Marcela from Chapter 14 of the first part of the *Quixote*. Blamed for the death of the shepherd-poet Grisóstomo whose love she rejected,

Marcela comes to defend herself. In doing so, she lays claim to a particular autonomy, and to the "voluntary" nature of love. In Fernandez's hands, Marcela's words become the words of Spain's defeated anarchists whose "demand" for the "impossible" echoes out of the grave – just as the pathetic poet Grisóstomo's words do when his poem is snatched from his funeral pyre.

VENDLER: Couldn't we also read this as the lament of the unread poet? Fernandez, more Grisóstomo than Marcela, has his poems snatched from history's silent grave by you, Menard. Otherwise, we'd never have heard him.

While Vendler speaks, Fernandez's hand once again rises from the coffin, this time holding an empty wine glass aloft. Menard sighs and, while responding to Vendler, he reaches behind his chair for a wine bottle, approaches the coffin, and begins to fill the dead poet's glass. However, looking offstage at Vendler the entire time, he does not pay attention to the glass, and continues to fill it. Wine over-flows all over Fernandez, who keeps his glass aloft until the bottle is empty. His hand and the glass then descend into the coffin.

MENARD (dumbfounded): You … no one can … you can't…. Look. (Long pause. Then, thoughtful.) "Poetry is a womb of souls which we as poets attend." That's what I'm doing here – attending to poetry. To its mysterious foundations in the unknowable and its impossible destinations outside our tiny intentions and mean-ings. It involves an intimate and unbreakable link between read-ing and writing, watching and acting, thinking and doing. That's what Fernandez did too. It's all we can do as critics (and poets). *Pay attention.*

At this exact moment, Menard notices that the bottle is empty, looks at it, looks down at Fernandez, shrugs and returns to his seat before continuing.

MENARD: Thinking, analyzing, inventing are not anomalous acts; they are the normal respiration of the intelligence. To glorify the occasional performance of that function, to hoard ancient and alien thoughts, to recall with incredulous stupor what the *doctor universalis* thought, is to confess our laziness or our barbarity. Everyone should be capable of all ideas and in some utopian future this will be the case. (Pause.) I simply want to enrich the halting and rudimentary art of reading – as Fernandez did too.

FERNANDEZ:

> I tell it you as all tales are told
> To wrest fiction from the dead hands of prose
>
> From dense histories
> Feeble cries
>
> Apparatuses for
> Forging chains
>
> To think of situations
> From books I haven't read
>
> Nothing but fire
> Steel pounding into shape
>
> Just as if it belonged
> To heretics
>
> The perverse and complicated
> Language of their authors
>
> Dear common these words
> Fallen out of context

The lights dim and the curtains close.

The Plebeian Cantos

Stephen Collis

Fernandez Fernandez Fernandez – it's the most
ordinary of Spanish names. And yet, in Madrid
in the early 1920s, the name was on everyone's
lips, and everyone was quoting lines from his
poem.

– Federico Garcia Lorca

It's the limits – or limitlessness – of poems and books that interest me most. What version of Wordsworth's *Prelude* is the "cor-
rect" one? Which iteration of Whitman's *Leaves of Grass* is most
"authentic"? Robert Duncan wrote *Ground Work* as "preparation"
for a poetry he did not live to write. Wordsworth's *Prelude*, too,
is an overture to a broader project that never quite arrived. It's
somewhere amidst these sorts of projects that I would situate
Ramon Fernandez's remarkably suggestive, never quite achieved
poetry to which, I contend, his "Variations," so ably translated by
Alfred Noyes, are a mere prelude. I do not think Mr. Noyes agrees
with me on this point – but he himself is of a capacious-enough
mind and heart to allow me my "dissenting opinion." Works like
Wordsworth's and Whitman's defy containment and singularity;
they are all their diverse versions and more – an incalculable poetic equation far greater than the sum of its contradictory parts.
Duncan's *Passages* poems perhaps come closest: they, in the poet's

words, "belong to a series that extends in an area larger than my work in them." It is that "area larger" that is the wonder in poetry – the suggestion, amidst poetry's inherent brevity, of a wider field of intellectual and emotional play the poem we read is a condensation of.

The evidence that the "Variations" were meant to take their place as a prelude to a longer more diverse work is to be found in the prose fragments and notes amongst Fernandez's sparse papers. The evidence is slight, but to me there is enough. Clearly, by far the largest portion of Fernandez's archive is missing – presumably forever lost. That there must have been more material goes without question – in a career that saw the poet writing (if not publishing), by all accounts, steadily, albeit slowly, from at least 1918 until his disappearance in 1936, a far larger archive than the few dozen pages we have is clearly indicated. Amongst these lost papers surely the material of a long, ambitious, modernist epic would be found. This longer, lost poem was referred to by Fernandez, in several places, as the "Plebeian Cantos" (in one instance, which Noyes assures me is spurious, it is called "The Red Album"). The "Quixote Variations" were meant to be its preface.

The notes upon which I base this claim are as follows:

The Quixote is the atrium – up and out from there. To unfold a 'Plebeian Cantos.'

The Real Work: a poem to sweep up all the most common experiences, to take language from the base, and lift it into poetry from there, so that all time's peasants and poor may sing spontaneously together, each voice audible and in harmony, of the great common cause of liberty.

Write a 'Plebeian Cantos' – an endless series to sweep up all my efforts as a poet, past, present, and future. Notes to follow. Prose and poetry. Open at the top and rising from the bottom.

They are in Fernandez's hand and somewhat difficult to decipher. They are on separate pieces of paper, though the first includes the draft of a fragment poem (with the title "A Spire"), as well as a tiny, pencil sketch of the *Sagrada Familia*, and the last is in a small notebook from which most of the pages have been torn and lost, but which also includes some material worked into the typescripts of the "Quixote." The notebook also includes, on its back flyleaf, a list of books read or to read, which includes Huidobro, Hernandez, Stein, Breton, and "the American Pound."

I have placed the prose fragments in this order to support my suggestion that all three can be connected: the "Quixote" is "the atrium" to "The Real Work:" the "Plebeian Cantos." Noyes and I both agree that the latter two passages belong together or refer to the same project (the second quotation is on a piece of torn paper that may very well have been removed from the battered notebook); the connection between these and the "Quixote" poem is where Noyes and I disagree, as he maintains that there is "no *material* connection between the statements." While this is true (the paper is clearly from a different source, and the handwriting suggests they are written at different points in Fernandez's writing life – the words 'Plebeian Cantos' are, for instance, added in different ink, over crossed out and illegible words), it does beg the question: what is the "Quixote" the "atrium" to? The movement indicated, "up" from the "Quixote," also, for me, connects the fragments (the references to the "base," "lifting," "rising," and the "bottom" all indicate an upward movement in-step with Fernandez's anarchism): this is more or less a quotation from the poet's own "Quixote:"

Naked I enter the bed
Of eternal war

My hands intruding love
Where blind fortune hates

I become the penumbra
Of powers, know

Death is certain
Inconstancy distracting rage

As they would order nature
While nature must into its own orders fall

And I would keep to the chaos of growth
Open at the top and rising from the bottom

What, however, does any of this matter? Who cares if the "Quix-ote" was meant to initiate a longer poem that we no longer have access to or which may never have been written? We read Words-worth's *Prelude* without reference to the absent "Recluse" it was supposed to introduce; what does it matter if we do the same with Fernandez? I think whenever we can have access to a more com-plete understanding of a work's place in an artist's overall prac-tice or project, our reading of that work will be greatly enriched. Furthermore, in this particular situation, the missing poetry may help answer what are for me nagging questions: Why did this ap-parently committed anarchist spend so many years working on poetic variations on that most literary and canonical of Spanish works, *Don Quixote*? Where in this long, formally innovative poem – seemingly immersed in the aesthetic concerns of radi-cal *modernismo* – are the poet's radical politics? Certainly Fernandez's political concerns make some appearance, but mostly in aestheticized form. Could it be that the "Plebeian Cantos" were meant to be that more overtly political work that the "Quixote" forms a merely ornamental flourish and aria to? Could it also be that Fernandez begins with Cervantes only, in the body of the missing poem, to overturn such quintessential Spanishness – to move Spanish literature from knights and quests (however parodically deployed) to the real work of class struggle, the liberation of the human spirit, and the implementation of *communismo libertario* (the goal of Fernandez's anarchist union, the CNT)? We may never have the answers to such questions – but the clues are tantalizing and the textual hints provocative.

I have a further theory regarding the fugitive "Plebeian Cantos." I think that many of the difficult-to-decipher notes that remain amongst Fernandez's scant papers are themselves also working notes, even, in some instances, drafts of the opening "cantos" of the long poem. I think – with some work, and some imagination – several cantos could be reasonably reconstructed. Their shape is still fairly indistinct. But this is the point of a poem intended to "sweep up" all experience, all an artist's work into a frameless frame.

The revolutionary poetics of the "Plebeian Cantos" can be found in two other prose fragments from Fernandez's papers. These two – written out in a careful hand on the first page of Fernandez's much-abused notebook – are set in direct counterpoint to each other, and the hypothetical poem's trajectory can be plotted through the intellectual space they map out.

Even narrative was once a revolution in form.

*

To wrest fiction from the dead hands of prose.

Here is the key to this poet's work – a work which we will never really be able to read, but which, through the tireless efforts of Alfred Noyes, we can at least glimpse the shadow of what we may be missing. The project is to tell a story – a deeply necessary story – but not to tell it in any expected or ordinary way. The novel is a thoroughly bourgeois art form; it is the product of capitalism, and reproduces the same inevitably. The story that needs to be told must come in a new form, which is simultaneously a return to the oldest of all forms – the story before it became ossified as "narrative." Or – and this seems closest to Fernandez's point – narrative, at its origin, is an entirely radical gesture – a leap out of a culture of idolatry and the Image (think cave paintings and stone carvings) into one of the abstract arrangement of events. This was one of the greatest of historical revolutions, equal to, and perhaps even coeval with, the invention of agriculture. "Civilization," as we have understood it throughout "written" history, is a story – is *Story* as such. Fernandez is sensing, and announcing, its end. Look where that story has taken us – to the brink of social and ecological collapse. For the tale of the tribe to be told now, he is saying, it must be told in a way that recalls that first opening of story, when narrative was a radical new invention. Fiction is still completely necessary – what is utopianism, what is the re-visioning of the future, Futurity itself – but the implementation of a fiction? But the new fiction we need now – stepping from the crucible of the twentieth century into the potentiality of the twenty-first – must be one that *wrests* the fictive "from the dead hands of prose" – from the dying paradigm.

This is what we still have not found – seventy years after Fernandez: a new mode of story. Our fictions are still imprisoned in "the dead hands of prose," and we still haven't escaped the prison house of the history we have been telling, the "civilization" we have been enduring, as it shreds lives, classes, species, environments – reaching a frenzy of self-destruction.

Fernandez's effort, to bring story back to the point at which the very technology of narrative was radically new, explains his choice of the "Quixote" as a starting point or "atrium" of his project. Cervantes's novel is widely recognized as the first of the genre – the first modern novel. Why not go back there to the place our dominant narrative genre began? It is interesting then that Fernandez focuses, in his "Quixote," repeatedly on those scenes and moments in Cervantes's great book in which storytelling and textuality is itself the subject: the destruction of Don Quixote's library; the discovery of the shepherd-poet's works; and perhaps most significantly, the complex existence of the narrative's "second undertaker." The story of Don Quixote, Cervantes tells us, comes highly mediated. There is the first history of the famous knight, which breaks off mid-scene; then there is another version of the story, found in the Alcana market in Toledo, "written in characters I knew to be Arabic." These our "second author," the narrator who has been reading and relaying Don Quixote's story to us, has translated by a Morisco "into the Castilian language," and on our story goes.

Fernandez, in working variations on the Quixote story, takes up a position as, really, a third or even fourth "author" of the Quixote. He enters into a space where story is communal, collective – where story is the very erasure of authors and authority. He works variations upon what turn out to already be variations, versions – inauthenticities. No true and complete story of the knight's strange adventures is possible. Interestingly, so too no true and complete version of Fernandez's "*Variaciónes*" is available to us. And – this could be the poet's point? – no true and complete version of the 1936 revolution in Catalonia is possible – its history also comes down to us second or third hand, highly mediated and saturated with the textures added by its various storytellers, its interested parties and government recollectors.

With Alfred Noyes stepping bravely into the fray, we now have another author, another "undertaker." The story of Don Quixote grows in complexity, layers, levels of mediation. The community bringing the tale to us extends. The work itself (what on earth can we now name "the work" – what body does it consist of?) has broken down all limits, all sense of definable shape and borders. Noyes gives versions of Fernandez who gives versions of Cervantes who (to enter faithfully into the fiction) gives us versions of Cide Hamete Benengeli (the author of the Arabic manuscript found in the market), who got the story from who knows where. We are drawn back back back into a shadowy place of story's origin in the revolutionary discovery of narrative – a possibly endless chain formed link-after-link-after-link-after....

from **The Autobiography of Gloria Personne**

Gloria Personne

Gloria Personne on Revolutionary Aspirations

I was born in a revolution. Out of a revolution. That's the fantasy I construct. 1968. Paris. I can yet come to be, as unfulfilled a promise as that year of my birth.

My poetic master was – even though I am not really a poet myself, my master was – a Spanish poet who died in 1936 (during another revolution) under mysterious circumstances (he's not the poet you're probably thinking of). Even more remarkable, perhaps, is the fact that this poet is known only to have published a single, fourteen-page poem (or fragment of a longer work). In the world of literatures, histories and revolutions, he barely exists! And yet he has his small following, his adoring disciples, amongst whose tiny numbers I can count myself. Perhaps we will replicate and expand. Perhaps we will disappear, unnoticed and exhausted, along with our hidden treasure.

When I first sat down to write about Ramon Fernandez, I found myself writing incomplete thoughts about the architecture of Antonio Gaudi. I began again. The second attempt resulted in about twenty spontaneous pages on someone named Dioscuro Galindo, arriving in Barcelona in search of Fernandez. I had begun what could only be a work of fiction. I scrapped that too. It was going to be harder than I had expected to approach the life and work of my master – a thin veil beyond which lay I knew not what.

Having never begun myself yet – all hesitation and waiting to be, all atrium and foyer, well into my 40s and of little account in any field as yet – I wonder about my obstructions. I have placed a revolutionary pressure upon myself: that art ought to change the world, dramatically, at a single stroke. Or at least aspire to that. What an incapacitating notion! In the face of such an imperative, others might throw off works at a frantic pace, handfuls of books or buildings or films, hopeful that one of them at least would do the job. I have the opposite reaction: debilitating terror; inaction; a tendency to always position myself as a neophyte, amateur, aspiring no one. I look at my feet, frozen to the ground, and I am barely able to breathe.

Nothing is as dreary as the actualized, I tell myself. The purely potential, the never fully seen, only half-glimpsed, keeps us forever on our toes, on the lookout for the rest of what we will probably never catch again but just so, just so, keep looking. The purely potential places the future deep in the past, where it continues to reside, awaiting event and fulfillment. This is what we mean by utopia. This is why we should resist the completion of Gaudi's Sagrada, just as we should Fernandez's poetry: they should remain a hint, a fragment, a possibility. A sketch whose full details might still come someday, in a revolutionary surge in the imagination.

I'm hiding here too, a sketch of a self. Can you see me yet? I sincerely doubt it. It doesn't stop me though.

Gloria Personne on Identity

I have had my identity stolen, experienced this crucial splintering, or dissolution. The bank contacted me, then the grocer from a nearby town, for a bill that had not been paid (I was living, briefly, in Brittany at the time, trying to write about urban planning from a small farmhouse amidst blue-green fields; it seemed best to consider cities in their absence). There was another Gloria Personne out there, doing things in "my" name, purchasing strange things on my credit. The police were unable to catch her; the abuse seemed to end, but "I" was never the same.

With the advent of the Internet I was able to Google this Gloria Personne; I found no references to myself, but did discover a "Gloria Personne" who had been a French dancer and died, via a stroke, in New Mexico in 1977. Another name, "Fran Obediente," did come up, as a known identity thief, now in jail in Portugal, amongst whose aliases was the name "Gloria Ann Personne." Whatever "I" was, I did not seem to exist – and yet these others – earlier "Glorias," dancers and thieves, who seemed to have lived my life for me – did. I could not get over this. I had been stolen before I had even been born.

I found, once, amongst childhood papers (school exercises, book reports, a diary from when I was 12), a short account of what I took to be a dream (undated). In the account, I was sitting alone in a small sailboat, crossing a sea at night. I sat at the boat's stern, looking backwards. There was no wind, no sound, yet the boat sped on, and leaves swirled in its wake, drifting down to alight on the moonlit sea. I described needing to watch, to see each leaf fall into its place. I cannot be sure – cannot recall with certainty – that I actually had this dream. It was too long ago – memory, imagination, or something I had read and so, absorbed? I could not escape the vision once found, it so completely obsessed me, so eventually I wrote a small poem about it.

It was only later that I realized – the vision was not mine! It belonged to another – an author, who had written the account that I had then copied out as a young girl – and I had, *unconsciously*, and in retrospect, *stolen it. I* was an identity thief! I, who am no one, stole from the past of others, to make myself up. It is one of the most common crimes – the historical invention of ourselves. It fills the pages of most of our famous "historical" and "biographical," and especially "autobiographical," works. Everywhere we look, the pretend are prancing in their imperial clothes.

This is, of course, what happens in fiction too: we steal identities and forge stories out of their pilfered lives. I tend to steal actual names – names of actual people from books I have read. Sometimes they were fictional people in the first place, but the theft seems no less a transgression, no less criminal. Fiction, as far as I'm concerned, must occur under the sign of a crime. The objects of fiction had some other life before, outside the work of fiction, the full extent of which we can only guess at as we hawk them on the black market of ideas.

Gloria Personne on Her Father

It has been said that my father owned a Paris bookstore. This is something of an exaggeration. It was, in fact, a book kiosk – one of those mobile carts or *colportages* one finds along the side of the Seine. Green and worn plywood. A collapsible awning. He was killed as the result of an argument over a translation of Homer – thrown by an irate American customer into the filthy river, beneath the grey surface of which he disappeared, never to rise above the rippling current again.

I have often wondered what became of his cart. I can recall perfectly the image of those folding shelves, the cupboard doors that would close over them to keep the books in their place when the cart rumbled down cobbled streets. My mother has no idea (an Englishwoman, we soon returned, with few possessions, to her home country). Would it have been impounded? Taken by the authorities, auctioned off perhaps? Another bookseller would have bought it, and my father's books would have continued to be sold, perhaps at just the place he had met his fate, another victim in Homer's catalogue of the fallen.

Gloria Personne on Architecture

My earliest memories are of buildings and urban structures. Going round and round the Arc de Triomphe in a little careening Renault. Fountains in public places. The Château d'Eau. Place Vendôme, with its ugly, imperial column (toppled during the Commune, they say, by order of Gustave Courbet). Facades reaching up high above my childish eyes, dirty and old, ornate and imposing. In London, it is Trafalgar Square and the pigeons – or else the tube – stations barely lit and filled with bustle. Places I sometimes confused with the Paris Metro, wondering where all the lovely white tiles had gone.

Most of these are not buildings as such. But they are built spaces. They are urban and social. I want meetings surrounded by stone. I want verticality as a backdrop to indiscriminate conversation, to the meeting of strangers. I want intersections of all kinds.

I think I love these open places – love to remember them, to recall the swirl of pedestrians, the urban loafers and *flaneurs* feeding stray birds – love these contradictorily open/closed spaces – because now I would not dream of entering them. Agoraphobia of a sort came with my late teens. I travel, still, between two cities – once a year in one direction, once in the other, contained in a small metal tube most of the time – and it is a painful and terrifying journey each and every time. But I seem to need that terror, just so often. When I arrive in the new city – Paris or London – I immediately disappear into ground-floor interiors from which I almost never emerge.

Is it always what we have lost, what we only dimly remember, that drives us? I would be an architect of public spaces, even though I am a shut-in reading books and watching the television. I do not go outside. But I ponder the outside, inside.

Today the television brings me the image of some public space somewhere on this burning world where a crowd has gathered by a low monument beside aging buildings. They are angry and the police are there in riot gear, their glistening shields (it has obviously rained recently) glinting in the light (of cameras? streetlights? the sky? we cannot tell). I have the sound off (as always) and watch the space, trying to reconcile the dimensions the different camera angles suggest. There is, I note, not enough verticality. Nothing soars. The crowd is dispersed. The police easily re-establish order.

I wonder about that word, agoraphobia. Fear of the agora? Of the space of public debate and true democracy? If this is its real meaning, then perhaps we have diagnosed the truly modern malaise: we are all agora-phobic now.

Gloria Personne on Boundaries and Trespassing

I was still quite young when my mother and I left Paris – but I have a few very clear memories of our life there. One took place at the Pantheon, outside in the square. I recall sitting on the paving stones and playing with a small stick (picked up in a nearby park), my father, I think – some adults I was with, at any rate – talking nearby. I was poking at some cigarette butts stuck between two stones. They were two tired and weary travellers, arctic explorers in white parkas, trying to make their way up a long crevice, hungry for the Pole. Poke poke – I helped them along. One became stuck, and I dug in with my stick to free him, the other explorer pulling hard on his rope. A cobble then came loose, and I was able to pry it up, surprised and exulting at this accomplishment. I could barely heft it in my little hands, curious to see the secret world revealed beneath, what subarctic wonders I would behold. The adults beside me stirred, turning in my direction. One said something, the others laughed, and then my father (I think) leaned down and said, "Careful how you wield that, little monkey, if you strike the right pose, all Paris will take to the streets and throw up barricades again."

That is, I believe, my mother's version of what was said. Told and retold after. In England we settled for a time in Kent, living with my grandparents in Mereworth. I hated the country, after playing in the streets of Paris all my preschool days. I was French, or so it seemed to me, and refused to speak this ugly English – even to my doting grandparents. I soon turned them against me, overhearing them call me, with no small amount of disdain and frustration, "the little frog." I would *ribbit* and croak as loud as I could, hopping around grandmother's legs, tugging her woolen English skirts or fraying apron hem.

Hedges were that strangest of wonders. They were an architecture I could not fathom. Their surfaces and lines suggested careful construction, but crawling beneath, I discovered a dense tangle of winding supports and beams running higglety-pigglety all over the place. How were they made? I seemed not to have suspected their organic "growth" or their relation to trees. My grandfather, after all, was a retired hedger who (I was repeatedly told) "put in half the hedges in Kent."

I found hedges to be powerful holders and revealers of secrets. I learned of my grandfather's long-ago infidelities while lying underneath the backyard hedge of the garden in Mereworth while my grandmother yelled, and my mother cried and cursed and wondered where I was. A permeable wall is excellent I think – for snoops, thieves, and storytellers. I like a wall you can inhabit – into which you can climb and dream. Mice must have wonderful lives. Not a space as such, in hedges we enter into the very boundaries that make spaces, the very mechanism of demarcation.

I also learned the story of my father's death from within that same hedge. Hedges became cages in which birds were the voices of absent fathers. Later I sought more solid walls.

Gloria Personne on Friendship

As something of a shut-in for many years (I can travel, now, with the help of medication), friendships were difficult to develop and maintain. They have also tended to be very literary, having letters and, now, email as their main means of transaction. There are two people I count as closest allies – neither of whom I have ever met, but with both of whom I have carried on an extensive correspondence. They are "friends" in every sense of the word. One is an architect, Vittorio Riente, professor at La Ciudad's Escuela de Arquitectura de los Andes. The other is a Canadian poet and translator, Alfred Noyes, author of *Compression Sonnets* and translator of Ramon Fernandez. I write here of this latter friendship.

I first came upon the name Ramon Fernandez (can I call him a friend too? He feels like one sometimes – but no matter how many times I write, he does not write back) when researching my first essay on Catalan architecture. One Josep Maria Puigal, writing on Lluís Domènech i Montaner's Palau de la Música Catalana, referred in passing to Gaudí's work as being (by contrast) "as incomplete as Ramon Fernandez's poetry." I investigated immediately. Nothing in any library or bibliography. But then I came across a reference to one Alfred Noyes, author of a single, slim volume of poetry (there is apparently another poem, a collaboration with Weyman Chan, entitled "Hi Weyman," but it has as yet not found its way into print). This Noyes, the biographical note indicated, was translating the poetry of Ramon Fernandez.

Sometimes one's friendship with the living is no different than one's friendship with the dead. At least, if one is a shut-in, this is the case: friendship is all writing and reading. What I appreciate most about Noyes is his role as lifeline. I would not know whether I was dead or alive, real or fictional, if it weren't for Noyes's letters and emails, which come to remind me, and call me to task. Gently prying me, white and shrivelled, from the crack between cobbles where I have become trapped.

Gloria Personne on The Past

All of my thinking – all of my being, perhaps – relates most strongly to the past. History shapes us all (this is no great revelation), but we live in a time that has forgotten history and forsaken the historical itself. This is because the past, like everything else, is so easily digitally altered. Everything is rewritten the instant it is written. I type a sentence that is historically true, then backspace over it, writing something untrue. Where were we yesterday? I wore scarlet and came off a plane in San Francisco, a young woman in a new country, going to university. Or, was I – was I the same young woman I was in another country, or, even before that, in another language? Was I? Who spoke my being? What did my name cover?

In San Francisco, I became Japanese for a time. Dressed as I thought a young Japanese woman attending Berkeley would dress. Studied Japanese history, especially the history of Nihonmachi and the internment, and struggled with a Japanese language course. Became a fan of Tadao Ando's architecture (really, my first formal interest in architecture). And then, at a costume party where I had dressed as a courtesan, a young Japanese-American friend threw a drink in my face. I sat outside on a steep street as the white makeup ran down my face and onto my red gown. We cannot escape the past, the travesties it has wrought, even in costume.

All of my thinking relates to the past – and yet I am certain of nothing *in the past*. I have heard contradictory stories from everyone. My mother met my father when she was a student studying French. This was 1968. But I was born (so my certificate says) in June of 1966. Was my father really my father? Or are the dates wrong? Was I born behind a barricade in 1968? Or did my mother, having given birth to an illegitimate daughter in England in 1966, flee to France, only to meet a man old enough to be her father, but willing to marry a young, single mother and adopt her toddling daughter?

I am making most of this up – but that is only because such familial lore – or the lack thereof – always seems made up, is always open to being made up. At some point I thought I should discover a dead and heroic ancestor. At some point I thought I would write myself into being, as the descendant of that ancestor. Now that I have begun to study architecture in earnest, after years of reading and writing about the subject, I think I may *build* myself – construct an identity and a history to inhabit. It's what we do. With ourselves, and others.

Gloria Personne on Being Unreal

Here's to the imaginary, the unlived, the fictional. What is architecture but a concrete fiction – a sort of three-dimensional choose-your-own-adventure? I want to build the architectural equivalent of Cortazar's *Hopscotch* – or write the novelization of Gaudi's Sagrada. Impossibility is what fiction should be for and about (leave realism for what happens on the way to the grocery story). But I know too that death propels and pursues our fictive impulses (where can we hide?).

In my own architectural musings I often think how the first buildings were made to house the dead, and that living chambers evolved as a periphery, literally and spatially, to this (see Katal Huyuk). So the human has always been building itself around the dead, for the dead. The story is just another such a structure built around the dead, so we can dwell in their proximity.

I have written one novel, badly, and left it for mice to eat. I did it the only way I knew how: quickly and without too much forethought or second-guessing. I entered a 3-day novel contest, drank coffee, avoided sleep. After 72 hours, there was a text for me to stare at, disbelieving. Now what? I gave it to friend so I could forget it.

What have I to worry about? *Qui est moi? Personne!* Still, every effort to write invokes its critic, tsk-tsk'ing, questioning the writer's motivation, decisions, skill, talent, authenticity, honesty. The ego aches so – aghast at its own petty fears and wants, and keening at the wounds it perceives itself to have received. If I reveal this thing someone will say, "Ah, she's a novelist, how sad and predictable, not an architect after all, how sad she missed her true calling, tsk-tsk."

When one feels not quite "real," one is always a child. Whether 40 or 20 or 80, one's unreality (or surreality?) is always a realm of childishness. You are free to imagine whatever you are – more free because you have never yet actually been anything. Let's be pirates. Let's be movie stars. Let's be revolutionaries. We are only as real as we imagine. I think every writer ought to be a fiction too. Why set boundaries? Only so we can project appealing beyonderies.

In the midst of my struggles with the very idea of writing a work of fiction, my one true friend, Alfred Noyes, wrote:

Consider the idea that you have a past – *the* past – to rely on. Specific details to console yourself. You will recall our meeting in Barcelona years ago – you on vacation, me researching Fernandez and generally brushing up on my pathetic Spanish (and Catalan!). It was in the Picasso Museum. You stood entranced in front of one of the Meninas variations. I came and stood beside you. We began to talk – about repetition, variation, translation. Picasso as Velazquez's translator – that's what you said. It struck me quite a blow. We wandered together, finding English our common language. I remember sangria and paella somewhere nearby in tight cobbled streets.

The next day I thought I was showing you the town, but it was you who wound up lecturing me about Gaudi, leading me through strange grottoes in Parc Guell, telling me about the great architect, sleeping at night in the unfinished Sagrada Familia. We rode bicycles everywhere in the sun. You could barely keep up.

This is all fiction, of course – Noyes and I have never met in person – but it was so good of him: he was trying to jump-start my imagination. I wrote back:

> What I remember is a little bookshop beside the Palau, and you buying a Catalan dictionary, when you were that confused about Fernandez's language. Or did you just want it – the little, black Vox Diccionari? We wandered across a narrow, winding lane from there, talking about god knows what, until we came to my apartment by the university. Spain is such a fantasy to me. There is nothing real about it, but it will not go away. But how can it be otherwise, when this very tale of our meeting is itself a fantasy?

I'm not sure what specific ideas Noyes gave me. But he set me off. Or set me free at least. Even the 3-day novel contest was his idea.

It is reading that I am good for – books and papers all over my little flat, books up to its ceiling, piled on top of the full shelves, on the radiator (turned off now that it's summer, of course), on the windowsill (the window dangerously open, ready to rain books down upon the Rue de Seine below), on the floor beside my chair and bed. Oh well. Heavy architectural books. Histories of cities and revolutions. Books that could kill by their weight alone. Or books you could build into a substantial barricade in the narrow street. But what is weight to the entirely insubstantial? As Noyes said, after one of my despairing tirades about writing difficulties, "This would be really terrible, *were we real people!*"

So here's to the imaginary, the unlived, the fictive. Long may we chase the fleeting images of ourselves down narrow streets!

Gloria Personne on the Recent Revolution in La Ciudad as a Subject for Architecture

> We came into the city
> Because we wanted a Gaudi
> To curve our thought's structures
> Towards liberty

> – Ramon Fernandez, "A Spire"

This is the title of an essay I should like to write, but am not yet able to write. Perhaps I will go to La Ciudad. Perhaps I will overcome my fears and fly into a nearby country, and then trek through the jungle to La Ciudad. Stay with Vittorio at the Esquela, follow the crowds singing and chanting through the streets, and talk with the planners sitting down to design a new city where there is no capitalism to shape its formation (what would structure this city? Empathy?). Maybe I already have my ticket. Maybe it's lying here beside the computer as I write these words of my incomplete autobiography.

In his essay, "Potentialité et la Architecture de Antonio Gaudi," Vittorio argues that a purely potential architecture is a real possibility – and is, in fact, the only possible revolutionary architecture. He describes (and provides some sketches of) a system of movable walls and prefabricated and redistributable modular forms via which the people living in a city can, surprisingly quickly, reshape the urban environment for their particular and immediate and fleeting uses and needs – only to (in a sense) "rebuild" the same space for different purposes the next day. A collapsible and redistributable public sphere. It would be as if the city were entirely made of semi-permanent tents, foldable and movable structures perpetually being dis- and reassembled. There is a design for a spectacularly vast tent to cover the new city's entire outdoor agora.

I can think of another possible model. There is a church in a small German town where they are playing a piece of music by John Cage that will take 639 years to perform in its entirety. Can you imagine? 639 years. How many generations is that? How many lifetimes? It is a normal score, but stretched out as far as possible, so that there are sometimes years between notes. The organ (recently refurbished) is 639 years old, and that is how they decided the length of the piece. Or else the church is that old – I can't remember exactly – anyhow, the organ can hold the notes as long as needed. So if a note must be held for a year, even more, the organ can do it, so if you visit the church you hear this steady background hum of the note. It never stops. The whole town though has committed itself, as a community, to the project. It isn't about individuals. It's about a community. It's a promise to and for the future – that there will be a future for this town, a future in which this music will still be playing, in which people living there will still be playing it and listening to it together.

I once heard of some musicians – in Africa, I think – who never stop playing. Some sort of myth in which the world will end if this tribe's musicians ever stop playing. So they play. When some get tired, others take over. Like substitutions in a game of football. They just keep playing. Some group of people somewhere in their community is always playing their music. This could be the basis of a performative architecture. Or the basis of all fiction, really. I begin writing and another takes over. This would suit me just fine.

In La Ciudad, the revolution began amongst the architecture students – that is, it began as a question of *design*. This means another world truly is possible: they are already drawing up its plans.

I need to go see those plans. I may even substantiate myself in the process.

An Eliastrel Filmography

Poco Yamamoto

Eliastrel is something of a mysterious figure in the world of contemporary film. Raised in Barcelona but possibly born in Romania (or at least having Romanian parents), Eliastrel – he has no other known name – lived in Paris from 1976, when he briefly studied at the Conservatoire Libre du Cinéma Français, until 1990, when he moved back to Barcelona (he is rumored to travel a great deal, though Barcelona remains his home). There are no verified photographs of Eliastrel; he has never appeared at a film premiere or festival or given an interview; and even his actors are coy about his identity (some even suggesting that they "were never sure who he was – who the director was," during an entire shoot). On the notorious set of *Chevengur* (1990), Eliastrel – or at least someone claiming to be the film's director – conducted all his interviews and discussions with the film's cast and crew by telephone, and even phoned in his on-set directions to his "assistant," who relayed instructions to the actors and camera crew – a practice that became increasingly frustrating during the gruelling eleven-month shoot.

If Eliastrel is the actor in *Un Perdador* (1981), as some have claimed (see the Maurice Debeau interview with Barbara Dodd in *La Variété*, November 1989), then he would also appear to have acted (as one of the less-skilled dancers) in the Raúl Ruiz film *Régime sans pain* (1984), and possibly – a very small part as the subterranean band's roadie – in Luc Besson's *Subway* (1985). Besson, certainly, has claimed to know Eliastrel well, "though no one," he remarked in the *International Herald Tribune*, "is actually Eliastrel's *friend*." This was after the controversy surrounding *Chevengur*, which Besson and others have urged both the studio and Eliastrel to release, to no avail. Maurice Debeau of La Bon Bête Films claims he is the only person, other than Eliastrel, to have seen the full version of the film, "the viewing of which I would not wish upon my worst enemy" (Dodd interview).

In Barcelona, Eliastrel has kept as low a profile as he did in Paris, even though this is the period of his greatest commercial (slight as it is) and critical success – with *El Album Rojo* (1997) – as well as the notable disappointment of that film's dystopian follow-up, *Interrupción 2319* (2002). Since that time, Eliastrel is rumoured to have been working on a documentary on the 2005 Paris riots, or what is possibly an extension of this, developing a new script for a film on global anti-austerity protests. But there is no confirmation and he is not working with any known production company or studio. Sometimes-collaborator Bruno Eguard claims Eliastrel is, even after *Interrupción,* "still obsessed with the fantastical, and futurity" (email correspondence with the author), while Vicente Aranda – on whose film *Libertarias* (1996) Eliastrel may have done un-credited work as a co-writer and editor – sums up his fellow countryman's reputation, calling Eliastrel "the strangest and most dangerous filmmaker in Europe."

Eliastrel's politics are blatantly revolutionary, and his disdain for the "industry" of film is readily apparent. However, certain of his mature directorial "signatures" – such as the virtual absence of women on-screen in his later films (their voices are sometimes heard off-screen, as in *El Album Rojo*), starting possibly with *Che-*

vengur (but also noticeable in Gabrielle's slide to the periphery of shots early in *Cabrone*, as well as her eventual elision behind the screen of the Cabrone's hospital bed) – has raised the ire of many feminists. Nevertheless, some, such as Eleanor Pardo, have argued that Eliastrel's films – particularly *El Album Rojo* – demonstrate the marginalization of women in revolutionary movements, and that such absence "contributes to the tragedy that Eliastrel reveals everywhere in the history of the left" (*Los Dramaticos*, January 2001). Other critics want to read something more personal, and more Freudian, into this aspect of the "mature" Eliastrel (his relationship with his mother, who reputedly spent years in a Romanian jail under Ceausescu, even possibly conceiving and giving birth to the future filmmaker there). But too little is known about the filmmaker to ground such readings in anything more than pure speculation.

Eliastrel is known for his manic and excessive productivity – much of which simply disappears into his obsessive process. He is said to have written entire books that his characters "might have written," or which appear as fleeting references in his films, including a volume of poems mentioned by one of the characters in *Chevengur* ("a faded and thin, green cloth-covered volume of verse celebrating the renaming of species of trees after the 1917 revolution," and written as something of a line-by-line response to Mayakovsky's "The Cloud in Trousers"), an entire sequel to Platonov's novel (apparently the entire novel takes place in a woodshed almost buried under winter snow) from which he adapted extra scenes for the same film, and a lengthy series of manifestos (with awkward titles such as "On the Necessity of Time Travel to the Victory of the Working Class") attributed to Ramon's bear, Luis, in *El Album Rojo*. Eguard, commenting on this eccentricity, has suggested that it stems from Eliastrel's fear of being "eternally minor," which propels him to create whole literatures "to give substance to his efforts," further noting the filmmaker's penchant for quoting a Paris chef as saying "if the food tastes terrible, make sure you serve large portions!" Eguard contends that this is false modesty, that the filmmaker is a classic case of an unrecognized genius, and that "there are always a host of other possible works that *could have been made*, and which swim like ghosts around the work you *do make*, troubling and fraying its edges; Eliastrel likes to include these, even if only in the process of making a film."

It is worth noting that Eliastrel's scripts are also notorious. They read, in Pedro Guizon's words, "like short stories. Nowhere does one have a real sense of dialogue or stage directions or dramatic setting. There is just fragmented narrative. Description. Thought. The rest we make up in front of the cameras. This, Eliastrel maintains, is more truthful" (personal correspondence with the author).

*

Dans la Rue (1978-9). 16 mm / 19 min. Silent. Black and white. Stock footage from Paris 1968, edited and looped. Repeated shot of paving stone leaving student's hand and arcing into a grey sky. First screened in 1982 at the gallery Passages des Neuveau Morts, Paris. Later released as a special feature on the *Mayakovsky* DVD (1999).

Un Perdador (1981). 16 mm / 39 min. Silent. Black and white. A man (possibly Eliastrel himself) removing various condiments from his fridge and pouring them down the sink. Moves then to the bathroom where he similarly empties a medicine cabinet's contents into the sink. Long final shot as the camera moves past the man, out the window, to peer into a narrow Paris street, which is filling with a fantastical shimmering liquid. Unscreened, but later released as a special feature on the *Mayakovsky* DVD (1999).

Les pyrénées (1981). 16 mm / 22 min. Silent. Black and white. The philosopher Walter Benjamin plays chess against an automaton in Turkish attire, high in the mountains at the border between France and Spain. Notable for its many strange camera angles – some using a variety of mirrors – and oddly framed close-ups of Benjamin (possibly played by Eliastrel himself once again, complete with large moustache and wire-rimmed spectacles) and the automaton. No chess pieces are moved until the last minute, when Benjamin's hand reaches out to knock his king over. The subsequent and final shot shows Benjamin falling beside the chessboard, apparently dead. (It should be noted that each of Eliastrel's films makes some direct or indirect reference to Benjamin or his work, leading some commentators to speculate that his films are, in fact, all discontinuous parts of one long film exploring the German's philosophy.)

Mur des Fédérés (1982). 16 mm / 23 min. Black and white. Soundtrack alternating between heavy metal and ghostly funeral music. Single shot: long, slow zoom across Pére Lachaise cemetery to the ivy-covered Mur des Fédérés. Screened at Passages des Neuveau Morts, Paris, 1982.

Les Coquillards (1983). 35 mm / 58 min. Black and white. La Bon Bête Films. Starring Mircea Brond, Alicia Morneau, Monica Brill. Characters speaking Parisian argot pick through garbage, wash clothes, peel potatoes, and jeer at police. Shot to look like a documentary, with many grainy close-ups, interviews, though without a linear narrative. An aging street person comes up with a design for a "cat piano," sells it to an entrepreneur, evidently becomes rich and is later shown hitting a dog with his large car. In the final scene, a woman tends to the injured dog in the street, just off-camera, during long shot of feet and shadows crossing the paving stones nearby (dog's yelps, woman's voice alternating between calming coos and loud curses).

Cabrone (1985). 35 mm / 96 min. Colour. La Bon Bête Films. Starring Raoul Piquet and Alicia Morneau. Story of a foul-mouthed dwarf, the "Cabrone" (Piquet), living in Paris in the 1920s and 30s and undergoing successive experimental surgeries to "get bigger." Morneau plays his nurse, Gabrielle; she falls in love with her patient, who rejects her because she is "too tall." Many scenes in the operating room, with cartoonish amounts of blood and screaming, close-ups of shaking hands gripping bedsheets, or of the Cabrone's slow recoveries, in which only Gabrielle's hands are shown, or her voice heard behind a curtain. There is little plot and scant dialogue. In the final scenes, the Cabrone climbs a ladder up and out of the sound stage, past boom mics and spotlights, his nearly mechanical legs clattering and shaking on the rungs.

Mayakovsky (1986). 35 mm / 73 min. Black and white. Documentary on the Russian poet, including long readings from his poetry, and an unidentified narrator. Film begins and ends with long montage of found footage of various suicides (the ending sequence a repetition of the opening, but in reverse). Shown at several festivals (the Letni Filmova Skola, Cinéma du Réel, daKINO) but unreleased. The film has enjoyed a second life on video (1990) and, later, DVD (1999), including several special features.

Chevengur (1990). 35 mm / 270 min. Colour. Unreleased. Adaptation of the Andrei Platonov novel. Starring Luis Pau, Mircea Brond and Sergi Tregebov. The film occupied Eliastrel for five years and was backed by La Bon Bête films (and supported by an Etant Donnés grant), which allowed for an extended shoot in the village of Dunino, outside of Moscow. The fall of the Berlin Wall (which occurred during the shooting) and other tensions added to the fraught atmosphere. Arguments over the film's length and final cut led to Eliastrel's "tucking it away in the can," and ultimately to his move to Spain. It is said that only one person (from the production company), other than Eliastrel, has ever seen the film in its entirety, though some bootleg shorter segments have made their way into underground circulation and can even be found on YouTube.

Abaco! (1992). 16 mm / 28 min. Black and white; colour. Silent. Unreleased. Found footage of vandalism (much of it by anarchists – some recognizable as footage from the 1936-9 Civil War) interspersed with shots of famous churches, apparently taken from a poorly made Turespaña film. Later released as a special feature on the *Mayakovsky* D V D (1999).

El Album Rojo / The Red Album (1997). 35 mm and video / 180 min. Colour. Canal Plus España. Starring Pedro Guizon, Chus Matteo and Bruno Eguard. Released in Spanish and, internationally, with English and French subtitles. Premiered at the Cannes Film Festival. The story of Ramon (Guizon), a failed poet and independent filmmaker, who travels through time (guided by a talking Russian bear) to various revolutionary hotspots, including Paris (in 1848, 1871, and 1968), St. Petersburg (1905, but not 1917), St. Georges Hill (1649 – this part of the film an homage to the 1975 Kevin Brownlow film, *Winstanley*), Cuba (1958-9), London (1391), Southern Germany (1525), Bolivia (1952), Spain (1936), Chiapas, Mexico (1994), etc. Ramon interviews key revolutionaries, takes cover behind barricades, is shot at, tear gassed, and arrested. Ramon may be based on the Spanish poet Ramon Fernandez, fragments of whose poems he occasionally quotes in the film. An unreleased first, rough cut of the film, under the title *The Second Undertaker*, has found its way into underground circulation in pirated form. It reveals that Eliastrel radically re-cut the original, so that perhaps only 45 minutes are shared between the two films, adding much new material – including the expanded framing device of the travels of the fictional documentarian, Ramon. The film garnered some positive, but mostly ambivalent reviews, and was featured in a few "best films of 1997" lists, though mostly in obscure art-house magazines.

Interrupción 2319 / Intermission 2319 (2002). 35 mm / 129 min. Colour. Canal Plus España. Starring Mircea Brond. Released in Spanish and internationally with English and French subtitles. Dystopian story of the caretaker of a church in a small German town where a single piece of music has been played for the past 319 years. Now, at the half-way point intermission, in a post-apocalyptic and desolate world, the caretaker must decide whether to carry on with the rest of the "performance." The film is almost entirely without dialogue. It was a crushing financial and critical flop.

The Transformation [a draft film treatment]

Eliastrel

Tangerine

Alison Wing slipped onto the balcony and stepped slowly, so as to minimize the creaks, down the wooden steps at the back of her house and into the narrow garden where tomato vines withered. It was early – even earlier than she should have been leaving to get to band before school – though if her mother noticed, which was doubtful, considering last night's blackout and her mother's complete dependence upon alarm clocks, that's what she hoped she would think she was doing. Don't be late – and don't skip!, she could hear her say, Alison's face contorting demonic, her hair replaced by flames. Maybe even breathe fire on her mother. She paused in the garden to do up her coat and insert her nose ring (the usual ritual she performed once out of the house and on her own) then walked into the alley. Alley – Ali – what her friends called her.

A raccoon sauntered away from the neighbour's garbage cans, one of which was lying on its side, its contents spilt on the broken asphalt. Newspaper with *Balloon Boy Hoax* headline. Grapefruit rind. Dead rat somebody probably killed with a shovel. Feminine hygiene. What a stupid name. Ali waited for the raccoon to pass out of sight. She wanted a cigarette. If only she could make her desires appear out of thin air, she thought, considering the grisly trash, but that's not the way it worked.

Streaks of light were appearing in a sky from which clouds rushed. A tree hanging over the alley began to catch this light as Ali watched, its autumn leaves a place where red, orange and yellow seemed to be meeting without losing their individuality. Tangerine? That might do. Ali ran her fingers through her black hair, starting at her right temple and moving back and down to the tips, willing a streak of that colour to appear. Tangerine. That's the colour she wanted for today. A long drag on her cigarette. She wondered if Santiago would like it.

Tents

Santiago held her hand as they walked up a busy street past windows displaying ridiculous things only the wealthiest of the wealthy could afford. They stopped to mock the poses of the sleek and shiny mannequins, their breath condensing in little clouds of laughter in front of their faces. Why didn't they have heads?

The traffic at the next intersection was intense. They were standing across from the Art Gallery lawn, and Santiago was pointing. Do you see it? What? The camp! Camp? Ali noticed some cardboard signs hung in a tree at the corner. Beyond them, she could see the blue and red forms of nylon tents and the slanting sheets of tarps, morning sun and dew lighting them.

They crossed, excited. What is it? What's it for? A protest, Santiago explained. A tent city, haven't you heard about it? It's happening in cities all over the world. Protesting inequality and shit like that.

As they reached the Art Gallery, they were greeted by a guy in a plastic Roman Centurion helmet and colourful clothes. Someone was talking into a microphone somewhere, the amplified voice thinly piercing the morning air. Tents of various shapes and sizes lined both sides of the path into the grounds. Santiago suddenly turned off the path, into the maze of tents, the mud beneath their feet, dragging Ali with him. She giggled. A seagull swept low over their heads, crying plaintively.

Santiago stopped at a dirty, green tent with duct tape patches. With mock ceremony, he stooped, unzipped the tent's entrance, and bowed in welcome. Ali curtsied and threw herself inside the tent. Santiago dove in beside her and they held each other on the bare floor, kissing and rolling onto their backs to look up at the light illuminating the tent's domed ceiling above them. The gull's shadow crossed. The world was almost perfect.

Mirror

The bathroom in the Wing home had a dusty pink sink, toilet and bathtub. The tub's enamel was chipped and scored, stained green under the dripping faucet. Old flower patterned (and peeling) wallpaper covered the walls. The mirror was nice and large, but it had a crack at one corner. It was held in place by four ornate-looking but now dirty plastic tabs.

Ali was looking intently in the mirror, and Santiago was at her side, watching her. Ali's mother was outside the locked door, knocking loudly and demanding she open it this instant – how dare she lock herself in there with that boy! Ali and Santiago laughed. Boobs? Santiago suggested, meeting Ali's eyes in the mirror. Fuck off, Ali shot back, jabbing an elbow in his ribs. Then she looked at herself seriously again. She leaned forward. She touched two fingers to her left eyelid, concentrating. Her eye became rounder, less hood-

ed, more olive than almond, as she brushed it – as though apply-
ing makeup – with her fingers. She touched the other eye and it
changed too. Santiago watched, trying not to laugh. Ali touched
her nose, holding it between her thumb and fingers, and it became
thinner, more pointed, upturned. Like Nicole Kidman, or maybe
Björk. She stepped back and Santiago considered her. Then they
broke into hysterical laughter.

Ali threw open the bathroom door. Mother, we are moving into a
tent downtown. Have the butler fetch my belongings! Ali's mother
stared at her, bewildered. Ali, what have you done! She reached
out to touch her face. Makeup? Take off that horrible makeup!
You should be proud to be Chinese – proud! Ali swore and ran
back into the bathroom, pulling Santiago with her and slamming
the door.

They resumed their positions looking in the mirror. Ali shrugged,
and touched first her left, then her right eye, changing them back
to the way they had always been. Almond, not olive. Better, Santiago said, nodding. I'm keeping the fucking nose though, Ali spat.
Santiago burst into laughter again.

Blackout

The morning Marika woke up with the power to change anything
she touched came after an extensive blackout the night before.
This was hardly noticed in the shantytown where she lived, where
there was no electricity anyway. But the men who were lucky
enough to pick up night shifts for nearly nothing in the factories
along the river were sent home when the power went out, and
they spoke about it over breakfast fires as though it were a very
serious thing.

Marika could hear their voices. She felt strange this morning, like something in her body had changed. Like something small but strong and rebellious had been born in there. She was used to strange feelings in her body, being in the midst of her teen years. But this was different. It was visceral, but good. A good, strong feeling. Like she had developed a new, unknown muscle overnight, and was flexing it for the first time. Watch out.

She listened to the water in the ditch that was separated from her head by a thin wall of corrugated tin. She listened to the men's voices outside, and her mother, most likely, stirring the breakfast pot – a metal spoon *ting'ing* gently against its side. The occasional crack of the fire. A dog barking.

Then she heard her uncle stir on his mat a few feet across the cramped space which her entire family – mother, father, little sisters and baby brothers, and uncle – all shared. She decided to get up before he did.

Penis

The first thing Marika changed was her uncle's penis. It might have been better if she had started with something less … controversial. But she didn't exactly think it through.

As he brushed past her in the narrow space between the family sleeping pads and the kitchen area of the shack, he casually grabbed hold of her ass with one hand, giving it a good squeeze. Not like he hadn't done that, and worse, before. But this time she spun around ferociously and in an instant, had grabbed at his crotch – almost a punch where there wasn't room to kick him. She imagined herself ripping that damn thing right off. He half-yelped, half-laughed. Then he pushed her aside and stepped back, a strange look on his face. Like freezing cold water from high in the Andes had been thrown on him.

Something wasn't right. He touched himself, and gasped. Gingerly, he pulled his track pants open and looked down between his legs. He fainted on the spot.

Gone

It took some time for everyone to calm down and understand what had happened. A large crowd had gathered around Marika's family's shack. Some of the older women, known to be healers, were invited to inspect Raoul's privates. They shook their heads or took a sudden step back, looking in Marika's direction with expressions strung somewhere between fear and wonder.

Marika's father was in a state. Cursing and yelling, he went off with his little brother and several other men, on their way to the hospital on the other side of La Ciudad.

Marika's mother, Diodora, sat with her daughter and several other women around the breakfast fire, staring at the flames or the ground at their feet. The older women came over, and two of them stood behind Marika, their hands hovering above her shoulders or close to her back without touching her, their eyes half-closed, their lips moving as they whispered prayers.

Diodora turned to one of the healers, who had inspected her brother-in-law. It's just gone? The old woman nodded. Like he'd never been born with one. Like a plastic doll. Diodora shook her head, stole an inscrutable glance at her daughter, then returned to staring at the ground.

Question

What would you change? I mean, if you could change anything –
what would you change?

Ali was leaning on the steps of the Art Gallery when she asked
this. Santiago was sitting two steps below her, leaning back against
her knees, smoking. A new friend, known only as Beelzebub, sat a
few feet away, tucking his dreds into a do-rag. In the courtyard below them, people milled about talking, waiting for something to
happen, or walking back and forth, in and out of the encampment
which now filled most of a city block with tents of various shapes
and sizes. People were unloading a pallet. The buildings rising all
about them. Things reflected in glass.

Santiago extinguished his cigarette on the steps and tilted his head
back, between Ali's knees, smiling into her upside down face.
Nothing. Really, Ali asked, a bit outraged – nothing?

Beelzebub chimed in. Everything. I'd change every fucking thing.
We got it all wrong. Profit? Don't need it. Everything free and
shared. Jobs? Don't need 'em. Everything's gonna be free anyway
– you give what you can, you take what you need. So – get rid of
governments, get rid of the unequal economic system, jobs, money, pollution, armies – everything. Poof. Start again with a clean
slate, you know? Just loving each other, taking care of each other.
That's the kind of shit I'm down with.

Ali laughed. What's gonna make anybody do anything, if you
don't get paid, or … rich or famous or whatever?

Beelzebub smiled, then gestured around them. We're all here,
aren't we? Anybody getting *paid* here? Anybody making any *mon-*

ey off this? Been here three weeks. Gonna be here for years – until everybody gets down with this shit!

Vancouver

It was fall and getting colder. Clear skies came after days of unrelenting rain, revealing fresh snow on the mountains above the city. Still people were camping. Ali and Santiago slept in their tent when they were too drunk or stoned to go somewhere warmer. When they did have their wits about them, they went to Santiago's place. He lived (some of the time, anyway) with his mother in the downtown east side, not far from the Art Gallery really. She cleaned offices at night, so they were completely alone if they went there between 11:00 PM and 7:00 AM. They would fuck and watch television, or eat what was in the fridge and then just sleep, getting some actual rest for a change. Then Santiago's mother would wake them up, shouting loudly in Spanish and they would get up hazily collecting clothes and Santiago's backpack and Ali's purse and silently move off into the streets of Vancouver while Santiago's mom kept yelling and waving her hands around in the air and generally telling them they were going straight to hell.

I could change her. Ali puffing as they walked down the street.

Santiago scowled. Into what? A toad? Don't do that shit. Don't even say that.

Ali shrugged. Suit yourself, dreamboat. She stopped and reached down into the gutter, picking up some soggy paper and a plastic coffee cup lid. Close up of this. Then it's a stack of green twenty-dollar bills. Ali rising.

Let's go eat – I'm fucking starving.

218

Trojan

Beelzebub introduced them to Trojan – the guy wearing the plastic centurion's hat. They had just finished the evening General Assembly, to which Ali had listened carefully (while Santiago slept with his head in her lap, the two of them on a blanket on the cold concrete, sitting in a circle with some sixty or so activists). Ali now stood with Beelzebub and Trojan, the blanket wrapped around her. Santiago had wandered off to their tent, or to find something to smoke or shoot.

Why do you guys call this a movement, not a protest? Ali asked.

Trojan, who often spoke at the meetings, was ready to respond. Tilting his toy helmet back and scratching his thinning, wispy hair.

Because we're not here for one day to demonstrate against one issue or problem. We're here to try to find solutions to ALL our problems, and we're going to stay until we figure out how to do that. And this is happening all over the world right now Ali, in thousands of cities around the world. And we all want the same thing: the way we're currently doing things, which only benefits the wealthy and destroys the planet's ecosystems, has to end, and we have to find a new way of meeting our needs and living our lives. It's a movement because we are here to stay, waiting for everyone to wake up and join us. To change the world, we need everybody on side.

Ali looked down at her feet, hidden in the folds of blanket and shadow. Change the world. Her feet were touching the world right now – could she change it? Or just bend down and place both her palms on the cold ground, like she was praying?

Pigs

Lydia Klein was walking from the barn back to the farmhouse. The sun was just beginning to lighten the wide sky, as it always was when she finished feeding the pigs. Just a hint of the beginning of blue. Even with the blackout and no alarm clock, she had awoken at the exact same time. Her father would be impressed – he was so sure she was a dopey teenager who just wanted to sleep all the time and who could barely keep up with her chores. She couldn't wait to see him standing in the kitchen, making his 5:30 coffee, convinced she was still sound-asleep in her room upstairs. Or maybe he was still asleep! She could see him, the clock dead-dark and silent beside his bed. The clock even bigger than his bed, toppling over on top of it. Wakey wakey, Mr. Pancakey.

Then she stopped in her tracks. Her boots moved ever so slightly in the mud. She felt different today, that was what was dawning on her. Really, strangely, different. She was not only awake, she was REALLY awake. She felt her skin beneath her clothes, every soft square inch of it, the cold morning air on her neck and cheeks, her hair in its individual strands. Like she wasn't really touching the air around her, the clothes on her body, the ground ender her feet. Floating. Vivid. Each cell its own living entity.

And that thing with the pigs just now – where she absently touched their bristly backs as they fed and, her mind drifting, changed them from pink to blue and back to pink again – that, she stood there realizing, that wasn't a dream. That was ... *real*. A word that seemed utterly made anew in this instance. She turned and ran back to the pens. There were the pigs, still pushing and shoving around the troughs. Pink. And dirty – but definitely pink. She hesitated, and then slowly reached through the slats of the fence and touched the nearest pig – an old sow she called Gladys (even though they didn't name their pigs normally, and Lydia only used the name inside her own head). *Blue*, Lydia thought. Gladys became the bluest pig you could imagine. Like a Smurf. Lydia's skin crawled. She was numbly aware of racing thoughts. *Pink*, she willed. Gladys turned pink again. *Big*, thought Lydia, and Gladys grew to the size of a well-fed cow, twitching and giving a kick in surprise. *Oh sweet Jesus, what the fuck is this?*

Power

As time went on, Lydia kept her power a secret. They had the largest, healthiest pigs in the State that year. And no one working on the farm was hurt. No one got sick. Everything Lydia cooked – she was helping her mother cook a great deal more this year – everything tasted … perfect. That's what her father said. Perfect. He was happier than he'd ever been, though that wasn't saying a lot. Fat, healthy pigs selling at top prices. Every sow swelling with a full farrow. His daughter getting straight A's in school.

Lydia kept her secret, even when the news began to break about the other girls, all over the world, who – it was *claimed*, the reporters and anchormen always carefully said – had suddenly acquired the power to transform things they touched. This story made the news near the end of the broadcast (Lydia's mother, despite being a farm wife, was a self-described *news junkie*), when light news items – wild animal sightings in the city, celebrities and fashion, a heart-warming piece about someone helping someone else for no other reason than that's what people did sometimes, despite it all – were covered with a bit of sarcasm and relief by the otherwise blandly dour broadcasters.

They were always teenagers, always girls. One, in Nigeria, was supposed to have made an oil field run dry (the oil company called

it an act of eco-terrorism and blamed an international environ-
mental organization that had been campaigning in the country).
A girl in Paris, or so her parents claimed, had made her family
unbelievably wealthy overnight (there were accusations of "in-
sider trading," and an investigation underway). Another – Lydia
couldn't remember where – had saved her parents' home during
a hurricane by turning an aging wooden shack into a solid stone
structure that, in the video footage, looked something like a squat
tomb.

Lydia would listen to these stories silently, wondering, as the television blared or her father muttered over the paper, her mother
saying something to him about college basketball. She made no
comment, asked no questions. Her skin tingled. She felt the air,
perhaps, on her skin, against her pores, which seemed to gulp like
open mouths, even though there was no draft and she was fully
clothed. She felt – powerful – ready to leap right out of her body,
for something she hadn't known about to leap out of her body.
But the power was all wrapped up in its secrecy, all about its being hidden from view. It was something special and something
entirely her own that she wasn't simply going to flaunt around like
a new dress or a college acceptance letter.

Love

A small, Mexican restaurant had opened in Lydia's hometown
the prior summer. No one seemed to be paying it any attention,
though *someone* was clearly eating there. Lydia was one who observed things, remembered details. So she had noticed, once or
twice, a thin and silent boy with dark hair and deeply tanned skin
– a boy around her age who could have been from her high school
but who clearly was not – who sometimes sat on a sagging and
battered wicker chair outside the restaurant, smoking and watch-

ing traffic pass. It was on her way to school, and the boy seemed to come outside at that time of day to watch the kids trickling past. (Seeing this in afternoon light, rural road, emptiness surrounding.)

One day when Lydia walked past, she saw the Mexican boy surrounded by some of the troublemakers from her school. A large boy named Dane had pushed him against the front of the restaurant, beside a window where white- and red-checked curtains hung. Gingham. Dane's free hand, Lydia noticed, balled into a fist at his side. White knuckles.

Lydia was pretty but plain, small and silent, and no one tended to notice her much. (We can imagine her because we have seen the movies.) She didn't have much interest in boys, nor they in her. But she now walked through the group of shouting and laughing young men, right up to Dane (who was as big as a football player, but wasn't one). He turned to face her, frowning. She stepped up close to him, calmly, gently, like his lover about to reach up for a kiss, or drape herself across his broad chest. Smiling, she raised her hand, and silently and softly touched her fingers to his lips. He was surprised at first, then tried to speak, but found he couldn't. Lydia's fingers slipped softly from his lips and, smiling, she walked away through the clutch of stunned boys. Dane was smiling now too. He turned to the Mexican boy and immediately asked for his forgiveness. Grin broad with affection. And then he asked his name.

George. Only it didn't sound like that.

Bigger

Ali and Santiago lay in their tent. It was early morning, after it had rained hard the night before. But now the sun was out, and beads of water rolled glistening down the outside of the green nylon. Ali watched water drop after water drop make its way down the tent's side while Santiago snored gently beside her. It was like seeing light travel, slowed to the speed of liquid. You could drink the universe this way.

She was thinking about Buggy Joe and Muriel and some of the others who were actually homeless – who had been in alleys – Ali – before the tent city went up, and who now felt like they had a sort of home. And a community. Friends who fed them and talked to them and joked around with them. A community which invited them in to discuss big things like taxes and democracy and corporations and the environment, who listened to them and valued them. Ali liked that – she felt it too – Chinese kid from East Van, dropping out of school to do drugs with her boyfriend – her single mother not giving a shit, really, except for appearances – but here people wanted her to hear what they were saying, wanted her to tell them what she thought, seemed not to care about anything other than the fact that she was, in fact, there.

Ali reached out to touch the damp, cold side of the tent. *Bigger*, she thought, and the sides of the tent spread out away from her. She stood and walked quickly towards the nearest tent wall, touching it again, *bigger*. The tent walls and ceiling shot out and up again – big as a circus tent now. Ali kept walking towards the side of the tent. *Bigger*, she touched it again, and it swelled and swayed out like a giant sail, like the inside of a giant hot air balloon, like a green shimmering sky, a stadium-sized tent covering the entire Gallery grounds, everyone there waking up in its vast circumference to marvel at the new, green and glowing sky she had made.

Nose

Hey Ali – your nose!

Santiago's beaming, round and tanned face. Nothing but a T-shirt, despite the cold.

Wha? – oh, yeah. Went back to the old country. Fuck Björk, anyway.

Limits

Ali ran through the tents as fast as she could, slipping in the mud. Mike had come to get her, and he ran just a few feet behind, catching her arm when she slipped. They reached the green tent, sliding to a stop. Several people stood around outside, including Beelzebub. Their faces were ashen, stony. Ali, her heart pounding, looked into the tent. Trojan and one of the medics – her name was Tanya – were inside, crouched beside Santiago. Tanya was working on his chest with her hands together.

LET ME IN! LET ME IN! Ali screamed. Trojan climbed out and Tanya sat to one side of the tent, breathing heavily. Ali dove in and threw herself on top of Santiago. He was cold, and his face was grey, almost blue. Where had his round brownness gone? His perfect round brownness? She held his face in her hands, kissing him and concentrating. Tanya reached out to touch her, saying she had to get out of the way, but Ali brushed her off.

Alive, she was concentrating, *alive alive alive alive alive*. Her tears were falling on Santiago's cold face, which she continued to hold in her hands, *round and brown not flat and grey, damn you*, but nothing was happening. Why? Why couldn't she change him back to the way he was? ALIVE, she shouted out loud. ALIVE damn you, you fucking asshole, WAKE UP!! WAKE THE FUCK UP!!

On and on she wailed, but to no end. She had found the limits of her power.

Spells

They would have to perform some kind of magic on Marika. Some ceremony. That's what one of the grandmothers said, while Diodora looked on, concerned, sitting on the ground where she had been idly weaving a basket, barely attending to the task. They would all leave in the morning and head up river, where the men harvested the chiquichique. Smoked fish would be offered to the elders, and they would drink fermented yucca.

There was a hole, one of the women began, telling one of their most important stories. A hole that had one of every kind of seed in the world. Inapirrikuli pulled out the seeds one by one, and they were transformed into all living beings – including Wakuenai and white men. He showed the Wakuenai books, but they did not want them. He then showed them bows, arrows, and canoes, and they said Yes, they could use these. When he showed the books to the white men, they took them.

Marika looked at the old women. How is this helping me, grand-mothers? Silly girl, one of them hissed. Tomorrow we will pray to Inapirrikuli, and drive the demons out of you. They will be seeds in the hole once again.

Marika looked at the ground. She did not want to go into the jungle. She did not want her demons driven out. *She* wanted to make a hole in the ground, and pull the seeds out herself, transforming them into beings, one after another. She would call them her friends. Comrades. There were things they would do together. Important things in the city outside the shantytown and outside the jungle.

Rodrigo

She was gone before anyone woke to work or cook. While the cats were still hunting skittishly amongst the trash heaps, wary of the wild dogs. For three days, she wandered the city. She begged. She slept in an alley, until a stinking man without pants drove her off. She was kicked and chased more than once, and threatened with all kinds of terrible harms. Then she found out she could turn dirt into manioc and cassava. Discovered doing this, she fed a small group of street kids younger than herself. They called her Maria, and said she was a saint.

In a café one day (she had turned some leaves into paper money, bought herself a dress and rented a tiny and decrepit apartment off Via dei Rojo, and thought that her life was almost perfect) she watched a group of young men talk in a close-knit circle, their chairs pulled together in a corner. One of them, who in his green beret looked very much the warrior (his hair was so long and dark), stared back at Marika for some time before pushing his chair away from the table and walking over.

You're Wakuenai, he observed. So what? Marika shot back. Nothing. Just … I noticed. I bet you know a few things. Yes, Marika said, I do, nodding towards the young man's table. She did not know what she was doing. It was all instinct and attitude. Bluff. How she was adapting to her new life. How the transformation made her feel. The young man removed his beret and ran his fingers through his long, curling hair. Why don't you join us. I am Rodrigo. Come. His hand extended. A smile on his face.

Plan

They had a map of La Ciudad spread on the kitchen table in the badly lit apartment. It was hand-drawn, and certain buildings were coloured in crayon – but it was a good map, and accurate. Filo, who had drawn the map (you could not purchase accurate maps of the city, in part because there was no tourist industry to speak of), stood back smiling like a proud father while Rodrigo, Juan, Tia, Berto and Marika stood or sat around the table.

Juan, ever the voice of reason, was scratching his head. But Rodrigo, even if we get inside the Banco – then what? We're just robbing a bank. You said we don't need money so much as recognition. Is this the way?

Berto made a guttural sound in his throat.

Look, Rodrigo began, we've gone over this. The Banco is American-owned. They are the whole reason our government is not bankrupt right now. They've bought this country. And they are simply paving the way for the oil and mining companies. The Banco is symbolic. This is like Robin Hood, right? We set up in the bank, like we're the tellers, and we just start giving the fucking money out. Giving it all away. That's how you get recognition. That's how you get people's attention. That's how you spark things – actions, insurrection. We take the Banco and hold it as long as we can, giving as much of it away as possible. Robin Hood.

Guns, Berto barked.

Marika has taken care of that.

No, Marika said. She stood looking at the map, hands of her hips. Everyone looked at her, but she did not return their gaze. I have a new plan. We won't be needing guns.

Caprice

Lydia could hear their voices on the other side of the door. Her father and the minister talking. Her name on her father's lips – which brought her quiet footsteps to a stop outside the door. Then the minister, Mr. Oakes, intoning. A young girl of that age, she is the very image of caprice. I don't think you should be too concerned, Byron. She will change. It's the other thing I'd be more concerned about.

They went on to discuss the *fact* that Lydia was a *lesbian*. She was puzzled by the word. Not because she didn't know what it meant. Simply because she hadn't ever bothered to consider the matter. She hadn't ever been in love, so who knew who or what she might love? Maybe she liked pigs better than people.

Lydia crept quietly away and went out back of the farmhouse where there was a row of poplars beyond her mother's vegetable garden. She watched the trees moving in the wind for a few minutes. What Lydia wanted, she decided, was books. Lots of books. She wanted to understand things. Big things. Like why the world was the way it was. Why there was this round object in space with people and animals living on it, dirt and rivers and oceans, hurtling along. Why on this object there were governments and television shows and singing contests and that sort of thing. There were only a few books in her father's house, and they were the plainest and most boring books you could imagine. She would have to find her own books. It was autumn. The poplars' leaves were drifting down and covering the ground.

Waiting

Lydia watched television with her father and mother, eating bland food (Lydia had lost interest in cooking). After the evening meal, she liked to walk in the fields west of their farm. It was up-wind, and you pretty much couldn't smell the pigs, and this seemed to let her thoughts leave the farm. Scale a few mountains. Touch foreign shores.

On Saturday, Lydia watched her cat, Chompers, catch mice in the loft of the pig barn. Chompers was patient. Lydia watched, and she was patient too. There was a lot of waiting in childhood. Lydia could taste the end of childhood. It was coming soon. School would be over. She hadn't learned anything, she decided. After school, her one ambition was to learn something. And to see something different. A city. Strangers. Maybe the ocean. She wanted things to change.

On Sunday, when the family was getting ready for church, Lydia announced that she would not be going. Her mother frowned. Not feeling well? Her father looked uncomfortable. It's OK, Dina, he said, glancing from his daughter to his wife, let's go. Lydia's mother hesitated a moment longer, then shrugged and let her husband guide her towards the door. Lydia went back up to her room to wait for time to pass.

Library

Along the line of poplars, Lydia collected leaves. She made a tidy pile of them in her hands, like a thick leaf sandwich. She tried to remember the names of books she had heard of. Not the ones they read in school – they were few enough, and boring. And she'd read them anyway. Then she remembered that, at tea after church once, Mr. Oakes had mentioned a book called *Moby Dick*. It was a funny name. The boys at school called each other dicks sometimes. Lydia shrugged and concentrated on her stack of leaves. Suddenly she was holding a thick, leather-bound volume. The gold lettering on its dark brown spine read *Moby Dick* and below this, the name *Herman Melville*.

Lydia leafed through the book. The smell of its ink. The sound and feel of its pages, which seemed not to want to part, but did so, gently. She sat down on the spot, her back against a poplar. And she began to read.

It was wise to make several books at once, before the leaves were gone, she decided. So she stopped reading after the first few pages (which puzzled and delighted her) and after having flipped through the pages to the back cover, she began to gather more leaves. A note at the back of *Moby Dick* led her to create *The Scarlet Letter*, *Walden*, and *The Poems of Emily Dickinson*. She took these four books, clutched to her chest, up to her room. This might have been the best day of her life.

Circe

Rodrigo wanted to fuck Marika but Marika did not want to fuck anyone, it seemed. The street children continued to come to her for food, and a priest had spoken to her after hearing something about *miracles*. There were definitely people interested in Marika's *case*, as they called it.

On the day of the Banco action, Marika stepped through the streets in a new dress and heels she was only just getting used to walking in (having practiced for a few days). She practically waltzed into the Banco building, touching the arm of the security guard as she passed through the door. He turned into a pig and ran off squealing into the street. No one outside seemed to care or take note. A small pig in the streets of La Ciudad wouldn't be a surprise.

Inside the Banco, Marika flounced around. Two other guards were posted in different parts of the large, high-ceilinged room. They watched Marika, her legs alive in the moving fabric of her dress. The second guard turned into a pig before he could understand why there was a pig running around the inside of the Banco. By this time, Rodrigo, Tia, Juan and Berto were in the building, along with some others who were part of their team (Filo was not amongst them – he said he would stick to maps). They herded the tellers together and Marika gave them each a kiss goodnight, on the tops of their heads. Sweet execution-style. All were soon sound asleep, locked in a vault.

Marika, Tia and Juan took up posts at the tills. Rodrigo made the announcement to the shocked and stunned patrons: Today, everyone that comes to the Banco gets as much money as they want. It is a gift – from global capitalism to all its faithful customers! It is time for a redistribution of wealth!

People were confused at first, and most who were already in the Banco left very quickly with frightened or puzzled looks on their faces. But as other customers came in to do their banking, and instead of doing what they wanted, the tellers asked them how much free money they would like, business began to pick up, and the Banco became a more lively place. The atmosphere became that of a party. Rodrigo read a poem condemning American imperialism. Light fell in beams across the building's colonial interior, like a temple, with tiny motes swirling in the sun. Marika was smiling like a fool. Only Berto seemed to retain a serious veneer.

Riot

Marika threw her heels aside so she could run faster. Tear gas canisters flew through the air above them like smoking comets. The
sound of gunfire crackled behind them again, though Rodrigo,
lifting his balaclava, insisted they were only plastic bullets.

The riot had broken out when huge numbers of police, armed like
a military unit, arrived at the Banco. The mass of people assem-
bled there, giddy with free money, had blocked the entrance. Berto swung into action, producing a gun from somewhere – even
though Rodrigo had said repeatedly (at Marika's insistence), *no
guns*. All hell broke loose: riot cops, tear gas, and bullets flying.
Somehow a restaurant beside the Banco was set on fire. The air
was full of bricks and other objects being pelted at the police lines.
Marika, Rodrigo and the others took off in different directions
when the police swarmed the ranks of the rioters.

Tia and Juan were arrested, though Tia was somehow soon released. A mistake on the part of the police perhaps. No one knew
what happened to Berto, but they feared the worst. Many people, who had been given money at the Banco, were beaten and
arrested. One woman died, though it was never explained how
exactly. Three buildings were gutted by the fire and several cars
overturned and destroyed. The next day, the local papers referred
to the incident as a bank robbery under the cover of an anarchist
diversion. No one spoke about the money being given away, the
Banco's recent expansion in the country, its ties to La Ciudad's
leaders, America or the multinational oil companies. The media
ignored a march the next day, organized by students at the school
of architecture, but the police were there in vast numbers, row
after row of armoured vehicles streaming through the city.

Touch

Rodrigo, Tia, Marika and some others new to their movement met in a secret location – a dark room there's no point in saying where exactly. Single lamp shedding little light. Some of the new comers were students. Eager, excited, but a little afraid too. A few of the others were young Wakuenai who knew Marika from the shantytown, or had heard the stories that were circulating, from what had been written about her in the papers.

Tia thought the Banco was a failure because of the violence, but Rodrigo was eager to plan their next action. They had learned much from this. They would be better next time. Plus, with Marika, they had a secret weapon the state could not account for. She was a gift, he said, from Che's ghost. It was because of her that they had to carry on, that they would win.

Marika shook her head. I can't touch everyone, you know. I can't touch everything. I'm one girl, that's all. Besides, you can't touch what we really need to change – you can't touch capitalism.

We touched the Banco, Rodrigo noted. Marika shook her head.

I'm getting this from you, Rodrigo. You told me. The whole system has to be changed, that's what you said. I don't know how to touch *the whole system*. Besides, what would I turn it into? A pig?

Tia broke the silence that followed. The factory workers, and the students too (here she gestured at some of those hanging on their words in the dim room), have been talking about striking. And the students had their march. They are organizing as we speak. We aren't alone. I hear, in Greece and other places – Egypt too – people are rising up against their governments. Against power, and money. Against privilege and exploitation. And now, even in America – in America, of all places – there are demonstrations. Big demonstrations. You can see them marching on the computer. I think, you know – I think maybe we *can* touch everything. We have Marika, but we have these others too. We have many voices now, in many languages. And all seem to be saying and doing the same things.

Emily

Book led to book. Lydia read *Love in the Time of Cholera*. She read Rilke's *Sonnets to Orpheus*. She read *Wuthering Heights*, and decided that she was in love with Catherine.

Snow covered the ground. One day, after she had arrived home from school, and getting down close in the snow, on hands and knees outside the kitchen window, she managed to just make out the impression of a bird's footprints. Little, pronged impressions in the perfect white bank, only visible from a specific angle, in certain light. Lydia wanted to write a poem, like Emily Dickinson. A poem about the bird's almost-invisible tracks.

At night, Lydia read while her parents watched the television. Only when the news was on, right after supper, did she put her book down to watch and listen.

Students

One night, the evening news was almost completely taken up with an incident at the state university, in a city not more than an hour from Lydia's farm. It was the university that students from Lydia's high school, if they were going to go to university (not many of them did), would often attend.

Students were holding a protest outside the administration building. There were many, many people, many signs and some camping tents in the background. The video showed a line of university police in black riot gear marching on the students. Some students were beaten with batons, and another clip showed a student cowering against a building and sandwiched between two shrubs, being pepper-sprayed. Just for a second. If you blinked, you might have missed it. Lydia had never seen or ever really heard of pepper spray. She saw the girl's frightened face, for that split second, clear as though she was standing right there, before the coloured spray came and they cut to another scene.

The story had cut to a university official speaking about the rules the students had broken. There was no other context. Lydia's father, who had been shaking his head through much of the segment, muttered – they deserved worse than that, if it was up to me, much worse than that.

Lydia watched silently. Then, when the piece was over and the elaborate weather forecast, complete with something called *the Doppler effect*, had begun, she returned to reading *Notes from Underground*.

Opening

Lydia had been keeping newspaper clippings, or writing down notes after news broadcasts, since she first learned there were other girls out there with *unaccountable powers*. Her mother said maybe she would be a journalist (which was what she had wanted to be, before she married a pig farmer). This always made Lydia's father scoff, though there was resignation in his laugh. Like his kid was weird enough already, what did it matter?

There was a girl Lydia read about in Mexico or South America (the story was very vague about the location) who was being called a saint. Like Jesus, it was claimed, she could produce food for the poor, transforming what she lay her hands on. She had now disappeared, and the Catholic Church was making a lot out of this, accusing a group of left-wing terrorists of kidnapping her, possibly even brainwashing her. Stockholm Syndrome. Another girl, in Canada, had come forward to say that she had the power *to transform anything into anything else*, and she wanted to offer her powers to her country's government, *to help the world*. She was going public now because she had received no response from the government. The only person interviewed, at the end of the segment, was a psychologist who specialized in paranoia, megalomania and other personality disorders.

Lydia stepped outside into the snow. The moon was up above the bare poplar trees, and the world around the farm had a silver-grey glow about it. It was almost Christmas, though Lydia didn't care or think much about that. There was a sort of opening in the world that had to do with more than the end of the year, more than this being the point when the days stopped getting shorter and started getting longer again. She would soon turn seventeen. She would graduate from high school in just half a year. And then she would be gone from this place forever, she was certain of that. She would be gone. Her future was an unending sequence of books, one blossoming out of another, a chain of flowers she was following or weaving together. *Anthology*, like the Greek word.

Things were going to change. She could see the opening. She could feel it. It was in her, or it was her. She was almost ready to walk right through it.

Illusion

Maybe she never had any power. Whatever that means.

Ali wandered along the edge of a vast sheet of multicoloured fabric lying on the grass in the park. Her eyes fixed on the air above the cloth, which rippled in the slight breeze, visualizing the giant arcing tent they would lift this huge quilt into. The space it would take up in the air, the ribbed supports holding it aloft. Its volume.

Power. She hadn't tried to *change* anything that way since Santiago. Now she was trying something else. For months working on this massive structure, working with many others, arguing and sewing, laughing with fabric lying across their laps, first in someone's living room, then in their backyard. Then a community centre offered a room free of charge on Thursday nights. It was like a sewing club. Now finally here in the park these past few days. To build a tent that many – hundreds if not thousands – could stand in together. Could gather in and speak, listen and be heard.

That dream was as fragile as tent fabric. And just as synthetic. But so it always is when making worlds. There was actual tent material in shades of orange, blue, grey, red, green and yellow. There were old sails. A rainbow parachute. Banner material. Tarps. Flags. Bedsheets. Thin cotton blankets. All sorts of things. The idea was that, once raised, it would look like a giant camp tent, all hooped arches, a dome pitched on the ground. A giant zippered entrance twenty people could walk through at once.

The art gallery was interested in it as a *site-specific piece* and had offered support. But Beelzebub hadn't wanted that, and Ali agreed. The others consensed. It had to be D I Y. It had to be a community raising its own tent. It had to be sudden and fleeting and done on their own terms. It wasn't for everyone but it was for anyone who wanted to be part of what was going on, who shared the community's goals.

Cops'll rip it down. Trojan, rolling a cigarette.

Ali shrugged slowly. I know. But we'll have it for a few days. And we'll all stand inside there together, looking up at the air we've raised above us, the shape we've given it. And that's worth it.

Then what?

Maybe we'll sing. Maybe we'll march.

Signs

Lydia walked across the campus under the September sun, a backpack slung over one shoulder and a worn novel that she'd just bought in her hands, a large yellow label that read *used* fraying on its cover. She was saying the word *feminism* quietly under her breath, over and over. Like she was whispering *bomb* at an airport.

In front of her were a group of students. Most of them knelt on the ground, writing on pieces of cardboard with felt pens. Someone was staring intently at a bullhorn in their hands, trying to figure something out. It made a sudden squawk, and the person jumped, and then giggled. Lydia stopped and watched, reading a sign over a boy's shoulder. The boy looked up at Lydia and smiled. He was a she, or so it seemed. A boy's haircut and clothes. But a girl's face and voice.

You like it?

The sign? Sure. What's going on?

Same old. Quietly, or not so quietly, changing the world.

Lydia smiled, looking around at the others. Another electric squawk from the bullhorn.

I'm Susan. The boy-girl standing now dusting off her jeans and extending her hand. What's your name?

Lydia still looking around, considering. Gloria. I'm Gloria, she said, looking into Susan's eyes and smiling. Glad to meet you, Susan.

Poem

Marika and some of the others stood in the rain outside the prison. Many, many others were inside – kettled and arrested by the dozens over the past few days as the marches had continued unabated, seemingly unaffected by the numbers being arrested, by the show of armed force. Many others had been taken to the hospital, and some no doubt to the morgue. Protesters had gathered there too this rainy evening, as they had each of the past three nights. Tomorrow, thousands would march again, and perhaps the soldiers and riot cops would meet them once again, arresting and smashing skulls, and tomorrow night, there would be this same vigil again outside the prison, the hospital and the morgue. Maybe Marika would be inside one of those buildings.

Or maybe tomorrow, the police and soldiers wouldn't show up. Or maybe they would join the demonstration and march beside the thousands of protestors. They would storm the parliament together, and the president would flee, his helicopter rising above the square and into a sky he would not ever return from. That seemed like a real possibility. Like a premonition. *Deus absconditus.* Every day they woke thinking maybe today they would join us, and the government would fall. How long could the state stand against numbers like this? It seemed absurd, inhuman. Then again, it was absurd inhumanity they were challenging, opposed to.

All this in Marika's eyes as the camera pans past her and around in a circle – the prison, rain falling, the vigil. As the small group stands in the rain and some whisper about who was arrested, who injured, who might have died. Why the police kept on opposing them day after day. How their numbers continued to swell. Students. Workers. Remarkable.

Then a voice lit up. A young woman who had joined the movement in recent weeks – a student from the university – who told Marika that it was her example that had finally driven her from the classroom and into the streets. That so many young women and men too were looking to Marika, young as she was (in part because she *was* young), for leadership, especially after they had seen her interviewed on a popular news program, which had debunked her so-called *miraculous powers.*

So this young student stood under a street lamp and raised her voice. You could hear the continent, dark and green, resound in the vowels her mouth made. You could hear generations of indigenous elders, the voices of Marika's mothers and grandmothers and aunties and great-aunties, echo like brightly plumed birds in the branching consonants. You could hear the seeds of everything germinating in a deep hole in the ground, about to be released. All this was timeless human and non-human sound. The words themselves were almost incidental, and though they were old words too, they were forgotten words, misplaced words, just now in the process of being rediscovered, just now becoming notable at last, more than seventy years after they were written. They were the words of the poet Ramon Fernandez.

Appendix

Stephen Collis: Two Poems

For Gloria Personne

What architecture holds
An eyebrow's arch
Above no one's eye?

Is it you who has left
These blue prints
On the beach for the sea to erase?

I walk towards the question of you
Somewhere in a South American city
Unfurling your pencil's art.

The dome above the abyss is lit
With incendiary ideas:
Is it you trying to corral them one by one?

Nothing is left but being alone.
The planet cools, Gloria,
Ready for you to plumb its unpredictable depths.

In Appreciation of Alfred Noyes

I make a pact with you
Alfred Noyes
An argument has its limits
Where a poem thankfully does not.

To have translated yourself
Out of the unknown language
Of another is your true gift
To have translated time
Where there was only timelessness
To have translated the space
Another body occupied –
You approach the place I begin
To ascertain the outlines of a poem
Neither of us will ever have written.

When we meet again the other side of words
No one will know who translated whom.

Acknowledgements

An excerpt from *The Red Album* appeared in *West Coast Line* 70.

Stephen Collis's essay "The Plebian Cantos," previously published in *Quixote Variations* (BookThug 2008).

Selections from "The Autobiography of Gloria Personne" previously appeared in *Memewar* magazine.

"The Theatre of Criticism" originally published in *The Capilano Review* 3.11.

The poems "For Gloria Personne" and "In Appreciation of Alfred Noyes" originally appeared in the first issue of *Dear Sir*, www. dearsir.org

Special thanks to the editors of these journals, to Michael Turner, Daphne Marlatt, Jordan Scott, David Chariandy, Andrew Zuliani and Jay and Hazel Millar.

About the Author

Stephen Collis is an award winning poet, activist, and professor of contemporary literature at Simon Fraser University. His poetry books include *Anarchive* (2005), *The Commons* (2008), *On the Material* (2010, awarded the BC Book Prize for Poetry), and *To the Barricades* (2013). He has also written two books of criticism, including *Phyllis Webb and the Common Good* (2007). His collection of essays on the Occupy movement, *Dispatches from the Occupation* (2012), comes out of his activist experiences and is a philosophical meditation on activist tactics, social movements, and change. Collis has read and lectured across Canada, the United States, and Europe. *The Red Album* is his first novel.

Colophon

Distributed in Canada by the Literary Press Group: www.lpg.ca
Distributed in the U S A by Small Press Distribution: www.spdbooks.org
Shop on-line at www.bookthug.ca

BOOK
PRODUCTION
WAR ECONOMY
STANDARD

Type+Design: www.beautifuloutlaw.com

13 14 15 16 17 · 5 4 3 2 1